An explosive force shook the ground...

Danielle protected Lucy, while Reece covered them both, shielding them once again. Debris rained down on them. This time from an explosion. Had the house blown up? Had that been an accident—a gas leak? Or intentional?

And Reece's sturdy military tanklike form protecting them from danger was turning into an unfortunate habit. Danielle fought the scream climbing up her throat as she tried to calm Lucy. Her daughter cried in her arms beneath Reece, who had pinned them down beneath him.

"Reece...?" Danielle tried to find the words, but her throat constricted. "What's going on?"

"It'll be okay. It's going to be okay." His confident words couldn't hide his concern. Still, Danielle couldn't remember when she had felt so safe. Even in the middle of this new terror, a sense of protection wrapped around her.

She could believe the words and repeated them to her daughter. "It's going to be okay, Lucy. Just wait a little longer."

Elizabeth Goddard is the award-winning author of more than thirty novels and novellas. A 2011 Carol Award winner, she was a double finalist in the 2016 Daphne du Maurier Award for Excellence in Mystery/Suspense, and a 2016 Carol Award finalist. Elizabeth graduated with a computer science degree and worked in high-level software sales before retiring to write full-time.

Books by Elizabeth Goddard

Love Inspired Suspense

Mount Shasta Secrets

Coldwater Bay Intrigue

Wilderness, Inc.

Visit the Author Profile page at Harlequin.com for more titles.

Taken
in the Night

Elizabeth
Goddard

LOVE INSPIRED SUSPENSE

INSPIRATIONAL ROMANCE

LOVE INSPIRED®SUSPENSE
INSPIRATIONAL ROMANCE

Recycling programs for this product may not exist in your area.

ISBN-13: 978-1-335-40521-0

Taken in the Night

Copyright © 2021 by Elizabeth Goddard

This edition published by arrangement with Harlequin Books S.A.

For questions and comments about the quality of this book, please contact us at CustomerService@Harlequin.com.

Love Inspired
22 Adelaide St. West, 40th Floor
Toronto, Ontario M5H 4E3, Canada
www.Harlequin.com

Printed in U.S.A.

But without faith it is impossible to please him:
for he that cometh to God must believe that he is, and
that he is a rewarder of them that diligently seek him.
—Hebrews 11:6

Dedicated to my Lord and Savior, Jesus Christ.

Acknowledgments

A big special thank-you to my writing friends and family
who support and encourage me and provide
story fodder for each and every book I write. Also,
I especially want to thank my King Jesus for giving me
this writing dream and opening the doors for me.

ONE

Small campfires glowed in the darkness, dotting the campground as Danielle Collins drove five miles per hour along the curvy, paved road. Her window down, she listened to subdued voices murmuring here and there as she passed campsite after campsite searching for her brother's flashy Tesla, which would definitely stand out.

She rubbed her tired eyes and tried to blink away the blurriness, exhaustion feeding into her mounting irritation. She'd spent most of the day traveling with her almost-six-year-old daughter, not an easy feat by anyone's standards, only to arrive at the Sacramento International Airport and learn that her brother would not be there to pick them up as promised. He'd invited them, after all. Persuaded. Convinced. No, insisted. But no, he wouldn't be there.

Instead, she'd received a text from John as she waited in baggage claim. He'd asked her to meet him at their favorite family getaway when they were kids. A guessing game. And she was in no mood.

Really. A campground?

Her texts and calls to him had gone unreturned.

She'd had to rent a car, one that she hadn't reserved ahead of time.

"Mommy, I'm hungry." Her daughter, Lucy, remained buckled in the back seat, where it was safest.

"Again? We just drove through and got you nuggets and fries—" Danielle glanced at the clock on the dash "—forty-five minutes ago."

"Okay. But I'm tired, too."

"Then close your eyes and go to sleep."

Danielle would absolutely wring her brother's neck for dragging her across the country and pulling this stunt. But this was not like John—and he had that in his favor. Was it some sort of crazy surprise that he was planning for Lucy's sixth birthday at the campsite instead of his house? Or did he want them to spend the time camping and reminiscing about their childhood because he had received a terminal diagnosis?

It was out of character for him to spring this on them. He was a planner, and he would have detailed everything she should bring with her for camping.

Was he in some kind of trouble?

That would also be out of character.

Shoving her hair back from her face, she spotted his vehicle and parked behind the Tesla. Blew out a breath and glanced in the mirror to see her faded skin and red, puffy eyes. She felt much older than thirty-three.

But Lucy would keep her young. Danielle glanced over her shoulder at the back seat. Lucy's eyes remained closed. Had she fallen asleep, after all? Should Danielle leave her in the car while she checked to see if this was even the right campsite, although what were the chances that another camper would have a Tesla?

She hated to wake Lucy.

Danielle got out and walked around the vehicle. Campfires filled the evening, and families walked. Kids played. Her apprehension melted, if only a little.

She was so not in the mood to travel across the country for a surprise camping trip. Her brother had truly lost his mind if that was the case.

Opening the door, she reached in to unbuckle Lucy. "Come on, baby. Let's go check on Uncle John."

Outside the tent, she said, "John. It's me. You there?"

The zipper flew up, and John poked his head out. "Quick. Get in."

He tugged her inside. He looked more haggard than she did, and Danielle instantly knew this wasn't about a surprise birthday party camping trip. She hadn't truly thought it was.

"Hey, Lucy." John crouched to eye level. "I can't believe how much you've grown, Peanut. I don't get to see you often enough, do I?"

"We come visit you once a year at Christmas, though. Last Christmas you made that hidey place for me in the walls. Will I get to see it while we're here to visit you?"

John's face twisted as if he contemplated the answer.

"I think you need a hug." Lucy hugged him.

John chuckled but didn't answer Lucy's question about her hiding place.

Danielle didn't miss the forced laugh. "What is going on? You were supposed to meet us at the airport." *We're supposed to have a surprise birthday party for Lucy at your house.*

She kept her voice even and telegraphed to her brother that she didn't want Lucy upset.

Lucy had been diagnosed with heart issues at two and had a pacemaker to assist with her condition. That's why Danielle just might blow a gasket. John had been badgering her to move here and live with him since her husband died two years ago, and she'd repeatedly refused him. She wasn't sure how she'd let him convince her to make this impromptu trip. Well, yes, she knew... he'd wanted to do something special for Lucy. But it was all last-minute, and him not showing up at the airport had thrown her off.

"Sorry." He gestured to the folding chairs. "Here, Lucy. Sit down. I have bags of popcorn for you to snack on. Some sparkling water, too."

Popcorn? At least he hadn't gotten junk food. Danielle tried to keep Lucy on as healthy a diet as possible, and she'd already had to resort to chicken nuggets and fries on this trip. But her child had to experience a little bit of real life, too. She wouldn't put her in a bubble.

Danielle tamped down her rising irritation and pulled a tablet and headphones out of her bag to distract Lucy while she and John had a *conversation*, then Danielle eased into one of the folding chairs. His tent was big enough for them to sit inside as though around a small campfire.

And that brought to mind a question. "Why aren't we sitting outside with a campfire like everyone else?"

"We would be too exposed." John eyed Lucy.

"Too exposed to what? And in that case, why not a hotel room instead of a campground? Why not your home?" Danielle watched her daughter eat popcorn and smile at the movie on her tablet. With the earbuds in, Lucy shouldn't hear their discussion. Any other time and Danielle wouldn't have offered the tablet. Camping was for unplugging.

"Please just tell me what's going on. Are you hiding? Are you in—" she whispered the next word "—trouble?"

He hung his head. "This will go easier if I just show you. Stay here. I have to grab something from my vehicle."

John stepped out of the tent. Danielle took in her surroundings. A small cot and sleeping bag. A backpack. Coleman stove. He'd always been an outdoorsy person, and that allowed him to get away from his job with a biotech company. She didn't even know for sure what John did at the company. Danielle had been too wrapped up in Lucy and keeping her healthy, which had been more difficult since Tom had died two years ago.

Outside the tent, two men spoke. John and someone else. A confrontation ensued as their voices rose, then…

Pop, pop.

Danielle froze. Had that been firecrackers or something…sinister… Something deadly? Heart pounding, she held her breath and waited while she watched Lucy, who remained absorbed in the movie on the tablet.

That sound was probably nothing. It had to be nothing and she was on edge for no reason. But that wasn't true at all. John was tense, and he was scaring her.

Danielle should check on him.

She started to stand when the tent rustled. Expecting John, she eased back in the chair. Instead of John, a strange man stepped through the slim opening and lifted a gun with a suppressor.

Before Danielle could even think to scream, he pointed the gun at Lucy while lifting a finger to his lips. "You scream and I kill her."

As if only just realizing someone other than her uncle had entered the tent, Lucy lifted her eyes to the man with a gun. Confusion and horror twisted into her sweet, innocent features.

Danielle rushed to Lucy and covered her daughter's mouth. "It's okay, baby. Momma is here. There's nothing to be afraid of."

Danielle would do anything to protect Lucy, including telling a huge lie.

Special Agent Reece Bradley shoved through the convenience store near the entrance to the national park. He headed straight back to the drink section and grabbed a bottled water.

After paying for it, he chugged it down inside the store, thinking he might need to add another bottle and some snacks. Working for the National Park Service Investigative Services Branch as a special agent, he'd missed both lunch and dinner, and the drive back home was another hour. Today had been a long, grueling day since a man's body had been found up by Foreman's Creek a few days ago. Reece had been called in to investigate the murder, but so far he hadn't found a lot of clues at the crime scene, or what was left of it, in the national park.

He headed back to grab another water and lingered at the snacks section, knowing he needed to eat his vegetables, because at thirty-five, he wasn't getting any younger, and he couldn't hope to keep his previous Navy SEAL fitness level if he resorted to junk food.

But junk food was closer and easier, and he was ravenous.

The door dinged, signaling that another customer had entered. The creeping, hurried cadence drew his attention, especially since it was coupled with deep, panicked breaths. That sound set him on alert and, without turning his head to gawk, he eyed the newcomer.

The woman spotted him, then turned on her heels and headed down another aisle.

Wait a minute.

He knew her.

It couldn't be.

Maybe she'd recognized him and was avoiding him. But he had to know. Last he saw her, she was in Kentucky with a husband and a baby. He strolled down the aisle and found her gathering up sacks of chips. Then she moved to the refrigerator and pulled out several pop bottles.

"Danielle…?"

She glanced up at him and forced a smile, an attempt at hiding the fear and panic in her eyes. She stood taller, too, as if that could change her terrified demeanor. A person would have to be blind not to see the fear.

What was going on?

"I'm sorry." Her voice trembled. "You've mistaken me for someone else."

Okay. He deserved that.

"It's me, Reece. You *know* it's me." He took a risk and stepped forward, reaching a hand out, palm open. "Danielle, what's wrong? Are you in trouble?"

"No." She fairly shouted at him, then calmer, she said, "No. I'm good. I don't know you. If you talk to me again I'll… I'll *call the police*."

He stared after her as she rushed to the counter and threw a couple of bills down.

To the cashier she said, "That's two twenties. That should cover all these chips and drinks. I don't have time to wait. Keep the change."

Then she fled, bursting through the front door. Her hands filled with junk food, she dropped a few bags on the way out.

Reece discreetly peered through the window to see the vehicle she got into. She appeared to be alone.

He rushed to the front. "Did that seem weird to you?"

"Very. You want me to call the police?"

"Not yet. I got it." Reece flashed his badge. "I'm going to follow up on it. You can give a statement later if that's required."

Concern for Danielle lodged in his gut.

Reece caught the license plate, and he stepped off to the side where he'd parked his unmarked SUV and got in. Then sped after her. He would follow her for now instead of scaring her off. He had no idea what was going on. No crime had actually been committed, but certain earmarks for trafficking and such couldn't be ignored.

He followed the vehicle, keeping a good distance between them so she wouldn't realize that he was following, but not so far back that he would lose her. If he got too close, he could cause her trouble, depending on the situation. Her safety was his priority.

The rear lights wove from side to side, as if Danielle was losing control of the SUV. Oh no. He needed to get closer. Looked like his intervention would come sooner than later. He increased speed. Her vehicle jerked to the right and headed for the ditch, where it plunged a few feet and abruptly stopped. The right back door flew open. A man gripping a young child jumped out.

He waved a gun around.

Oh, Danielle...

Pulse thundering in his ears, Reece turned off his vehicle lights and pulled off the road far enough back that maybe the man hadn't noticed him yet. Reece had been a Navy SEAL before working as a special agent for ISB, but in all his experience, he had never had to face saving someone so close to him. Myriad strategies raced through his brain about how to get Danielle and her little girl away from the armed man without putting them in even greater danger, because they were already in harm's way.

Danielle rushed around the vehicle toward the man, who clearly used the crying child to his advantage, and the sound could tear Reece's heart open.

Keeping to the trees and shadows, Reece crept forward, his gun ready.

"No, please, don't." Danielle's cries of desperation stabbed through him. "I beg you, let her go. She can't endure this. I'll do anything you ask, just…please… let her go."

Reece pushed away the crushing pain in his heart that her cries brought on and focused on the task. He took in his surroundings. The silent night around them on the lonely mountain road. No other vehicles had driven by. Dusk shifted in into full-on night as he slowly approached. Only the light from the ditched vehicles revealed what was going on, but it was much too dark for Reece to take a shot at the man.

Reece continued his approach and sneaked around. He could come up on the man from behind, but he still couldn't get a clear shot without risking the child's life.

The man tugged the whimpering child behind him. "I should cut my losses while I still can."

"What do you mean?" Danielle asked, but the fear in her tone said she understood all too well.

Suddenly he pressed the weapon to the girl's head

as if he'd grown tired of the effort of managing those he'd abducted.

Reece was out of time.

He stepped out of hiding and aimed his weapon. "Police. Drop your gun."

Squeezing the child tightly, the man twisted the gun at the child's temple.

"Mommy!"

Danielle took a step forward. "Please…"

Reece didn't have a clear shot. He couldn't take one without risking the girl's life.

"He left something with you," the gunman said. "You have twenty-four hours to find it. I'll be watching. Double-cross me and I'll kill you and your little girl."

The man held the child as a human shield, pointed his gun at Reece and fired.

TWO

The events unfolded before Danielle as if in slow motion. Reece had ducked behind a tree and avoided the bullet meant for him.

Lucy's big blue eyes widened and fear twisted her sweet face. Their abductor held Lucy up in front of him as a human shield. Danielle's scream seemed to come from somewhere outside her body as she rammed into Reece to throw off his aim so he wouldn't return fire. She couldn't let him accidentally shoot her baby girl, though at the same time, she understood Reece was trying to save her little girl. To his credit, he didn't shoot.

And the man thrust Lucy forward as he backed away, fired his gun in a warning shot, then dropped Lucy as he fled into the woods.

It all happened so fast and yet so slowly.

Gasping, Danielle rushed to her daughter and lifted her crying child into her arms. Pressing Lucy's face gently against her shoulder, she ran her hand through her curly blond hair, weaving her fingers through the softness. She could have lost Lucy. "It's okay, baby. It's over now. It's…over."

Reece had disappeared into the woods. Chasing their

abductor, no doubt. Danielle tried to calm her pounding heart, for Lucy's sake.

If I'm calm, Lucy will see that and she'll calm down, too.

She wiped Lucy's tears away with her thumbs. "You hear me, Lucy? It's over now. We're safe. Mommy's here."

Danielle had always been overprotective. Lucy would probably be fine. But this kind of crazy gun shooting and kidnapping business was stressful for a healthy person, much less a fragile child with a heart condition.

A figure stepped from the woods, and Danielle tensed, ready to protect Lucy.

Reece Bradley. He'd come back alone, so he must have lost the gunman. She blinked a few times, taking him in. He was still the strong, confident *GQ*-worthy good-looking guy she'd been hard-pressed to forget, but she'd moved on, thanks to Tom and Lucy.

Still, she hadn't forgotten his last words to her years ago.

She could hardly believe it when she'd seen him in the convenience store. Danielle had thought her desperate hidden message to Reece to *call the police* had gone unanswered. But apparently he'd followed her instead. And he carried a gun. Was he the police now?

"Are you okay?" He stepped forward and held his hands out while keeping his distance, approaching like he feared she might run again. To be fair, she had lied to him that she didn't recognize him in the convenience store and had rushed away.

Thick emotion preventing a verbal response, she could only nod. "You saved us. Thank you. Oh, thank you."

Danielle couldn't prevent the rush of tears.

The next moment, Reece's arms wrapped around them both. "I thought you were acting strange back there. Like you were in trouble. Of course I had to make sure that you were all right."

Releasing them, he slowly stepped back and studied them. Danielle held tight to Lucy, unwilling to relax for even a moment. Her little girl finally relaxed against her, the terror vanquished, and now she peered at their big, handsome hero. Danielle wasn't ready to look into Reece's steady gaze and instead watched her daughter for any sign of anxiety. Lucy took in their protector, her gaze reflecting the smile in her lips as admiration bloomed in her eyes.

"My name's Lucy. Are you a police officer?" Lucy asked.

"It's nice to meet you, Lucy." His grin was bright— for Lucy's sake, she was sure. "I'm an investigator with the National Park Service. A special agent. But you can call me Reece." Reece flipped open his badge to show them. "And I need to call the local authorities so we can get a manhunt on for the guy who abducted you. Let's get you into my vehicle where you can be safe while you wait. I'll call for a wrecker for the car you were driving, too."

Danielle got into the passenger seat and held Lucy in her lap. After what they'd just been through, she had no plans of letting go any time soon. Or at least until Lucy was required to sit in her own seat with a seat belt.

Reece got in on the driver's side, pulled out his cell and called in reinforcements. When he was done, he looked at Danielle, his forest green eyes filled with concern and regret. "Is there someone I can call for you?"

Grief lanced through her. No. There was no one. She

and Lucy had no one now. "My brother, oh… John. Oh my… My brother was shot back at the campground." Danielle covered her eyes, then dropped her hand. "I can't believe I haven't already told you. I was just so… I was just scared for Lucy. Please call an ambulance for him. Oh, I hope someone already found him and called for help."

"It's okay. You've been through an ordeal. Now that you're catching your breath, you're remembering what happened. You remembered your brother."

Reece made another call and learned that John had been discovered and an ambulance already called.

Thank You, God. Oh, thank You.

"Oh, I'm so glad. Except…is he…is he dead or still alive?" Tears tried to surge again, and her heart beat erratically. She might need a pacemaker like Lucy if she had to take much more than this. She pressed her forehead into Lucy's soft hair and breathed in the faint and calming scent of strawberry-watermelon shampoo.

Compassionate eyes looked at her. "I wasn't given that information, but I was told someone would find out and let me know. Let…you know. Let's hope for the best. As soon as I can, I'll get you to the hospital and we'll find out about your brother. While we wait for the county deputies, can you tell me what's going on?" Reece's tone was smooth and calming.

"I don't know where to start."

Lucy shifted in the seat and stared up at Reece. Danielle wished her little girl would fall asleep so she wouldn't have to listen in on the tale and relive it all over again.

Reece studied them. "You know what? Let's wait on that." His eyes flicked to Lucy and then to Danielle, and he nodded as if he understood they should talk when Lucy wouldn't be listening.

Relief flooded her. She appreciated his understanding more than he could know.

A few moments passed, and Lucy snuggled against her. She whimpered a few times as if she was having a bad dream, and Danielle wanted to wake her. At the same time, she didn't want to wake her. Too many opposing and conflicting thoughts came at her. She couldn't think clearly.

"Are you sure you're okay? Did he hurt you?" Reece spoke quietly. "I mean… I could call an ambulance for you while we're waiting."

Danielle squeezed her eyes shut and shook her head. "He didn't hurt us. Not like that. No." Not physically, other than to abduct them, but perhaps psychologically. A definite yes on that, but it could have been so much worse. She got the sense the man was more desperate than violent. His hands shook when he held the gun. Why had he shot John, and what did he want from her? *Oh, John…*

Maybe he hadn't intended to shoot John, because he was clearly after something, but they'd fought. She recalled the argument outside, the grunting and wrestling. Then the gun must have gone off on John. Maybe the man hadn't intentionally shot him.

She hadn't learned what any of it was about, and now John could be dead. No, Reece was right. She should hope for the best. John had to be alive.

Because if he wasn't, she had no idea what she was going to do. She had no idea what the man wanted her to find. She only had the fear that remained with his warning—if she didn't turn over what the man wanted in twenty-four hours, she and Lucy could be killed.

For some reason, the man thought John had shared information with her. He kept harping on that during their mad escape from the campground. Even if he hadn't meant to shoot her brother, he'd targeted Danielle. Maybe he'd entered the tent believing he would search it and find what he was looking for, but found Danielle and Lucy.

Danielle had maintained she knew nothing, and she'd feared he would kill her and Lucy. He would likely kill them even if she had the information he needed—after all, he'd shot John, intentionally or not. He'd shot the only person who could have given him the answer he sought.

Sirens grew louder, and the flashing lights reflected in his mirrors. It was about time. He knew Danielle wanted to get to the hospital to check on her brother—he hoped the man was still alive—but Reece needed to stay here to speak with the deputies about Danielle and Lucy's abductor and where he'd taken off in the woods. While he also needed to take her statement, he would wait on that until Danielle had Lucy in a good situation. He wouldn't subject Lucy to more trauma if he didn't have to.

He had never been more relieved in his life than when the man dropped Lucy and took off. For a few moments, Reece had feared he would witness a terrible scene, and that he had bungled a rescue. But the two were safe in his vehicle, and though he remained guarded and on task, he breathed a little easier.

"Wait here," he said. "I need to tell them about the

gunman. Show them where he took off. After that, I'll take you somewhere safe. You'll need to be prepared to tell your story."

"I understand." She pressed her face into the top of Lucy's head.

Reece got out to meet up with the local county sheriff's department and was glad he didn't see his brother Ryan. He didn't want to bring up that Danielle was the woman in trouble.

The wrecker arrived to tow the car; for now, it would be held while the evidence techs gathered what they could. Along with deputies and park rangers, additional agencies were called in to search the woods. Maybe this man who shot Danielle's brother was the same man who had killed someone else in the region, though the two events could be unrelated. Still, what were the chances two men had been shot in the park in the same week?

Stranger things had happened, including the fact that Danielle was sitting in his vehicle.

He pinched the bridge of his nose. *God, in all my imaginings, I never dreamed I would see Danielle again, and it breaks my heart that it's under these circumstances. Please help her though this, and help me know what my role should be.*

He didn't want to leave her to go through this alone, her and her little girl, but Reece doubted Danielle wanted him to be the one to walk through this turmoil with her.

His cell rang, and he answered. "Bradley."

"I got the news you requested. John Steele is at the hospital. He was alive when he was brought in. Alive and critical. That's all I know."

Good news coupled with some bad news. His shoulders sagged.

At least he knew what to do next. He got the okay to remove Danielle and Lucy's luggage from the vehicle she'd rented, then stowed it in the back of his. Then he climbed into the driver's seat of his SUV. "I just got the call about your brother. He's alive and was in critical condition when he was brought in. That's all I was told."

Her brows furrowed with her smile. "He's…alive?"

"Yes." Reece started his vehicle. "I'll take you to see him now, then maybe we'll have a chance to find out what's going on."

"Oh yes, please take me. Oh God, thank You, God."

When she started crying, he fought the urge to wipe her tears away. While he steered back onto the road and headed toward the hospital, he let her words echo through him.

Thank You, God…

She hadn't been a Christian back when he'd known her before, and in fact, neither had he. Or at least he hadn't been following that path, though he'd believed God existed. He would ask her more about that if he got the chance, but right now he was still on duty and in a law enforcement capacity, so he wouldn't get personal with her.

On the forty-five-minute drive back to civilization, they still didn't discuss what had happened. Instead, Danielle sang and hummed uplifting spiritual songs to Lucy, soothing her little girl's troubled mind and heart. Reece found himself moved with the sound of Danielle's voice, his soul comforted as well. Maybe Danielle had been singing to herself, too.

In the parking lot, he got out and offered to carry

the sleepy, dead-weighted child for Danielle. When Lucy didn't object, Danielle accepted his offer. Carrying Lucy, he escorted Danielle to her brother's hospital room. The man had already undergone surgery and had been moved to his own private room. Tubes connected him to various machines. Monitors beeped.

Danielle stared at her brother. Lucy shifted in his arms and looked at her uncle.

"Mommy, is Uncle John going to be all right?"

Uncertainty lingered in Danielle's gaze as she studied her brother. "Of course, honey. But we should still pray for him." Danielle took Lucy from Reece and carried her over to a small sofa against the window, where she also found an extra pillow. "In the meantime, why don't you get some rest? This has been a long, hard day, and an even longer night. You need to sleep. Okay, sweetie?" She kissed Lucy's forehead. Satisfied that Lucy would sleep, Danielle relinquished her proximity to Lucy and edged closer to John's bed.

A doctor stepped into the room and introduced himself.

"I'm John's sister, Danielle. Please tell me he's going to get better."

"He's stable, but I'm afraid he's in a coma."

He's in a coma... At those words, Reece had the distinct feeling that the butt of an AR-15 had slammed into his gut. Still, he kept his composure even as memories of waking up from his own coma rushed over him.

Danielle's lips turned downward, and she wrapped her arms around herself. "A coma...for how long?"

"That's just it. We can't know how long someone will stay in a coma. Right now let's focus on the fact that he survived two bullets and he's alive. We can hope and pray that he'll wake up soon."

Danielle stared at her brother, unshed tears surging in her eyes.

"Do you have any questions for me?" the youngish physician asked.

"Not yet. No. I'm… I'm just in shock." She shook her head and touched John's arm.

Reece wasn't sure that it mattered if the doctor knew everything Danielle had been through tonight after John was shot, but he hoped the physician would be gentle with her.

"If you think of something, I'll be around." The doctor nodded and left.

When he'd heard the word *coma*, Reece had experienced a visceral reaction. He'd been in a coma and then rehab for two years. When he'd woken up, all he could think about was getting back to Danielle. More than anything he regretted telling her to move on without him. Not to wait for him, but then again, he hadn't been ready for a commitment and asking her to wait would have been selfish.

Still, he'd tried to find her, and when he had, she was married and had a child. She'd done as he asked and moved on, but he hadn't found moving on so easy.

He compared every woman to Danielle. What a fool he'd been to walk away from her. But he couldn't think about his mistakes and the past. Right now, he had to focus on solving this investigation. Why had John been shot and Danielle been abducted? What information was the gunman after? Though this seemed like the entirely wrong time to do it, there was no point in putting the inevitable off.

Closing the hospital door, he positioned an extra chair over on the far side of the small room and gestured for Danielle to take a seat. She lifted a brow.

"I need to hear the story now, I'm sorry. You need to tell me everything before you forget the details."

"You mean before I end up in a coma, too—or dead?"

THREE

She hadn't meant to snap at him. Danielle exhaled slowly and rubbed the back of her neck. "I'm sorry. I shouldn't take my frustration out on you."

"No need to apologize." He held up a finger, letting her know he would be right back, then stepped out into the hall.

She moved to sit in the chair. From here, Danielle could watch Lucy sleep and John rest if that's what one was doing while in a coma. Could he hear them? She'd heard stories about those coming out of comas being able to hear conversations and being completely aware of their surroundings. If that was the case, then it was like John was imprisoned in his own body.

"Oh, John, we need to know what this is about. We're all in danger. Please, please wake up. Please tell us what he wants," she whispered. She wiped the moisture from her cheeks.

Reece returned with a folding chair, which he situated close to her, but not too close, then lifted a pencil and pad.

"Okay. I'm ready to take your statement."

In the quiet hospital room, Danielle told Reece everything that had happened from the moment she'd made the decision to fly out to meet John to the moment Reece had saved them from the crazed gunman. All this she shared while watching her brother and keeping an eye out for Lucy, who slept, albeit fitfully.

"What about the moment the vehicle swerved into the ditch? What happened then?" Reece's tone was gentle and patient.

"That…that was on me. Lucy was crying and started screaming. That's quite out of character for her, but I think she was panicked and scared. No matter that I tried to comfort her. In the rearview mirror I saw him lift his hand to slap her." Danielle closed her eyes and hung her head. "The thought of him hitting Lucy filled me with so much rage. I couldn't allow that to happen, so I swerved to prevent him from slapping her, then lost control of the car."

Reece nodded. "I understand. You wanted to protect Lucy. And it turned out well, considering you're here now, instead of with the abductor."

Pursing her lips, she nodded. "That's everything."

He flipped the notepad closed and lifted one corner of his lips. "You did well. You've been through so much tonight. If you'll excuse me, I'll be back in a few minutes."

Now where was he going? She rose and moved to stand against the wall near her sweet baby. Reece returned again and held steaming cups in his hands. A sack hung from his wrist. He set the cups on the small table and dumped the contents of the sack. M&M's and chips.

He brought her one of the coffees. "Would you like M&M's or chips?" He gestured to the junk food and shrugged. "I couldn't help but notice that you grabbed a lot of chips at the convenience store."

"Dropped half of them, too." She gave a half-hearted chuckle. The whole situation seemed surreal.

"But you didn't get to eat them." His lopsided, compassionate grin warmed her.

Also surreal that he was the guy to come to her rescue. Life had thrown her a few curveballs over the years. Why not another one?

"Oh, that wasn't for me. Not for us. The man said he was starving and hadn't eaten all day. He was sweaty and shaking. Maybe he was getting low blood sugar, I don't know. But he wanted snacks and threatened to harm Lucy if I didn't make it quick. I didn't know what he wanted or even how much, so I grabbed as many bags of chips as I could." She looked at Lucy with her blond curls hanging over her face and preventing Danielle from seeing if Lucy was truly asleep. But Danielle could hear her breathing, see the slow rise and fall of her body, and in those familiar sounds and movements, Danielle knew Lucy was in a deep sleep. Her sweet daughter was exhausted and probably terrified, too. That thought ripped through her. She hadn't missed that Reece's presence had a calming effect on Lucy, and for that she had to be grateful he'd been the man to help them.

Danielle didn't want to admit just how terrified she'd been, and still was. The gunman was still out there. She had twenty-four hours to find something. What, she didn't know. Reece needed to know what he was dealing with, taking her and Lucy on. He needed the whole story, or at least the part she was willing to share. Danielle sat on the small sofa next to Lucy.

"Lucy is… She has a heart condition."

"I didn't know."

Of course he didn't. How could he? But he didn't tell her how sorry he was, and for that she was grateful. She didn't want sympathy or words that made it sound like Lucy was less than any other person.

The man from her past suddenly moved closer. He crouched in front of her and took her hands in his bigger, stronger ones. "I'm sorry this has happened to you, Danielle. Please tell me what I can do to help you."

Her hands trembled, and she retrieved them, drawing them up and under her folded arms—a protective stance, though she hadn't meant to telegraph just how scared she was. She'd expected him to tighten his hold and keep her hands, but Reece was gentle, and she had nothing to fear from him. Except maybe memories.

"You heard that man who took us. Who shot John. He thinks John gave me something, and I have to find it. He's coming for us. I have twenty-four hours to find whatever it is that he wants. I have no idea what it is. He wanted me to give it to him. Well, how am I supposed to do that, even if I find whatever it is?" Danielle rocked her head back and closed her eyes. She had to calm her swirling, chaotic thoughts. She dropped her head again to look into Reece's eyes. "His demands made him seem out of his mind. Like he wasn't thinking clearly. But the way things unfolded, it's obvious my brother had information—in his head or otherwise. He was hiding and he was scared. As for what you can do for me, if you're willing, Reece, well, you can get this man and lock him up for what he did to my brother." Her voice nearly broke at the words. She had to pull herself together for her daughter's sake.

She glanced at Lucy.

"And the trauma he's put you both through." Reece stood and folded his arms.

She'd never heard him like this—so gentle and caring. Or at least the Reece she remembered from long ago had seemed noncommittal. This guy here and now was a different person and yet the same. How could that be? Was it because he was now in law enforcement? Had some event while he was in the Navy SEALs changed him?

"I'll do my best to find out what's going on. Know that I'm here for you, Danielle. I'll be here to protect you and Lucy, too. I give you my word. But in terms of finding the answers, I'm going to need your help."

She shrank back against the couch and closer to Lucy, pulling her daughter's feet up into her lap. "I don't know what I can do to help. Lucy…you can see she needs me."

He nodded, understanding in his eyes. "You can help me to help you. Now that you're here and safe without a gunman breathing down your neck, maybe you'll remember something. The man said that John left something with you."

"But that's just not true. Maybe John was going to leave something with me, but we hadn't gotten that far in our conversation."

"Okay, then." Reece pressed his hand over his mouth. "Let's say John did give you something, only he hadn't told you yet. Where would John have hidden whatever this man is after?"

Lucy cried out, and Danielle shifted so that she could put Lucy's head in her lap. "It's okay, baby. Just a bad dream."

Her daughter turned her face to Danielle, though her eyes were still closed. "When are we going to Uncle John's? He has a surprise for my birthday. You said so."

Danielle inwardly groaned. As it turned out the surprise was for John to be shot and in a coma, and for them to be abducted. Danielle lifted her eyes to meet Reece's. His brow wrinkled as if he understood the new kink in their situation, then he slid the chair by the door closer to her and Lucy.

Of all the surprises, seeing him again and having him back in their lives, no matter the circumstance, was the biggest surprise of all.

"We'll go to Uncle John's soon, sweetie." Danielle frowned even as she said those words. Wait…that would be too dangerous. "Or we'll find a hotel," she corrected. She glanced up at Reece. "I'm so exhausted, I haven't thought far enough ahead. I haven't thought what to do after coming here to see John."

"I'm going to get you two somewhere safe. You might have been wondering why we're just hanging around here. Or maybe you had planned to stay here in this room with John, but I doubt it, because knowing you, you want a normal place for Lucy."

"Um…"

"As in a safe house. I'm getting you to a safe house. You heard the guy. You're not safe until we've taken him down."

Danielle's world was shifting under her too quickly. She wasn't sure what to say, except, "While that sounds well and good, I think it's imperative I get to John's house as quickly as possible."

Reese studied her, a finger over his lips. "You think you can find what this man wants there? I would think that if it was there, he would have already found it. But he didn't, so he came after John and then you, and he believes John gave it to you. So you still want to go there?"

"I realize John fled the house and was hiding, but maybe he did that before he was able to get the information. The item. The flash drive or key, whatever he wanted." She shrugged. "I don't know, I just feel the need to go there and see for myself."

"That can be arranged, but after—"

"No, before I go somewhere safe. I need to look tonight. As soon as we leave the hospital."

"Okay, but as I mentioned, I have a feeling that John's home has already been searched. I had planned to take a look around the house myself, tomorrow in the daylight. Considering what you shared, I might get a warrant to search inside the home as well. But these things take time."

"Still, tonight, Reece. Will you take me there?"

He eyed Lucy, his concern for her daughter apparent. Reese excused himself to answer his cell and moved out into the hallway. As Reece insisted, John's home had likely already been searched and there was no telling what they would find, or rather not find. Danielle knew that. Taking Lucy there, too, was a risk, but their lives were already at stake, and Danielle wouldn't leave Lucy on her own, or trust anyone else with her safety.

No, she had to go look at the house. Maybe something there would jar her mind, or serve to remind her of something that John could have told her or any kind of place he might hide something—because he hadn't shared a thing with her.

She hated every moment of this. She allowed her gaze to linger on Lucy.

Oh God, how am I going to protect my baby through this? How do I keep her a happy and safe little girl when she has already experienced more trauma tonight than any child should ever experience?

When Reece stepped back into John's room, he headed right for Danielle. A few feet away, he peered at her, his intense eyes unsettling her insides like they had years ago. Okay. That was unexpected.

"I've secured the safe house for you."

How had he done that so quickly? Relief surged through her. The urge to rush to him and find comfort in his arms, even if only for a few moments, overwhelmed her, but she remained where she was. He was a help to her in this moment, but nothing more, and she would do well to remember that.

Oddly enough, this man from her past who had pushed her away and out of his life seemed to be the answer God was providing.

Now all Danielle had to do was trust.

A monumental task.

Reece had requested an officer from the local police department be posted at John's room, and he waited with Danielle until someone was in place. He'd also asked for an officer to wait for him at John's house for added protection, but the local police department didn't have the staff to watch an empty house. Reece was just one of a few special agents covering the entire Pacific region, which included several states. They investigated poaching, missing persons and even murders and did that without the resources available to other agencies, but in this case, Reece had taken on a woman and child in danger. Special protective services could be arranged, but he wasn't so eager to trust their lives to someone else. He needed to keep them close since they were intricately tied to his investigation.

And maybe other, more personal reasons played a role in his decision.

Once again he carried Danielle's sweet daughter, exiting the hospital. The little girl wrapped her arms around his neck like it was the most natural thing in the world, her soft curls spilling over his shoulders. She'd immediately burrowed into a special place in his heart.

Back in his unmarked SUV, he drove an exhausted Danielle and sleeping Lucy to John Steele's house in the Redding suburbs. Reece was glad that, during the thirty-minute drive, Danielle had fallen asleep, too. It was two thirty in the morning, after all. Her hair spilled over her shoulders, golden strands like her daughter's, and, at the moment, one might never guess what she'd been through tonight.

Her gorgeous tresses and those striking blue eyes had drawn him in when he'd encountered her years ago, and tonight, her eyes had drawn him again and threatened to anchor him by her side. His heart ached for all she had gone through tonight, and that she had lost her husband two years ago. More concerning was that her child struggled with heart issues. He wasn't sure that going inside her brother's home was the best idea, yet time was of the essence and they needed to find what had been passed on, or hidden and was now lost.

On the approach to her brother's home, he noted the affluent neighborhood. Next to him, Danielle stirred and yawned.

"I'm sorry. I didn't mean to fall asleep." She rubbed

her eyes and peered out the window. "We're almost there."

"Yep. So…what does your brother do? Last I remember he had just gotten a doctorate. I realize that was several years ago."

"He works for a biotech company. He has a biology doctorate and some other degree I can't pronounce. I'm embarrassed to say I don't know all the details of his life or his job. When he talks about it, it's so over my head that my eyes usually glaze over. Now that I think about it, he stopped talking about his job a long time ago."

"It's okay. It's easy to see that you've had your hands full."

She shot him a glare. Oh no, she was sensitive on the topic. He'd have to clarify. "With a wonderful, beautiful child. Lucy is amazing."

Her features softened. She was definitely defensive and protective about her little girl. He didn't blame her. He would feel the same if he had a child, especially one as mesmerizingly adorable as Lucy. Her name totally fit—to Reece, she looked like a Lucy.

"You passed his house. You missed it."

"No, I didn't. I'm just taking stock of the neighborhood. Looking to see if anyone might be waiting near the house to ambush us."

"Are you serious? You don't think that could happen, do you?"

"I don't know. I'm not sure that bringing you to John's house is the right thing to do. But I don't see much choice if we want to get to the bottom of this before it's too late. I could look through the house myself."

"But you wouldn't know what you were looking at."

"Give me some credit."

"Okay. Sure. You're an experienced law officer, but you know what I mean. Nothing would stand out to you like it would me. I know my brother, okay? Besides, I feel safe with you, Reece. It will be okay."

She emphasized the burden to protect them that had fallen to him. "Fine. Let's make it quick."

"We'll be in and out. I promise. We won't stay long. If we don't see anything obvious, then we'll leave and come back during the day and search the place with a fine-tooth comb."

He blew out a breath. *God, please let this not be a bad idea.*

As he steered along the street, a few lights were on in bedrooms or living rooms—someone up late reading. Getting a glass of milk. Whatever. But Reece saw nothing out of the ordinary along the street. No suspiciously parked vehicles. No one lurking near the houses or in the shadows, though his headlights created eerie shadows all on their own. Finally he pulled in front of the house and parked at the curb.

"Stay here." He got out and planned to clear the home first. "I'll be right back."

A door shut behind him, and he whirled.

"I'm coming with you." Danielle held Lucy in her arms. "I'm not sitting out here alone for him to take us again."

Guilt flooded him. "I didn't plan to leave you long enough."

He would only take a few minutes to clear the house. Taking her into the house could put them in danger. That's the other reason he'd wanted an officer here. Someone to either clear the house or wait at his vehicle with Danielle.

"It's okay," she said. "Let's just get this over with."

Reece glanced at Lucy but said nothing, hoping Danielle would understand his silent question. Did she want Lucy to see whatever they came across?

"She's asleep. I'll keep her comfortable, and she'll sleep through it."

With the key Danielle had given him, Reece unlocked the door and entered, his weapon ready. He wasn't surprised to find the home ransacked.

Danielle gasped. "I… I thought this might happen, but I never imagined. The place is…obliterated."

Reece remained tense. "Except the walls."

Danielle stood close to him. "Right, the walls are still standing."

"And not much more," he said. "Wait here while I clear the house."

He rushed through and cleared each room, flipping the lights on as he went. "It's all clear. Are you ready?"

Before Danielle could reply, Lucy peered at her. "Mommy, do you think that my special hiding place is still standing?"

"I don't know, sweetie. Why don't I check that out." Danielle held Lucy out to him. "Here, could you hold her for just a second?"

He hadn't expected the offer and took the little girl with one arm. She settled comfortably against him, but he held on to his weapon in his other hand. "What are you doing?" he asked.

"I have an idea about Lucy's hiding place."

"Okay. Let's hurry and get you somewhere safe. I doubt we'll find what the man was looking for here if he hadn't already found it." Then again, Danielle could be the only person who could find it.

Danielle started down the hallway then turned and gasped. "Do you know if they found anything in John's car? I can't believe I forgot, but he had been going to get something from his car to show me. How could I have forgotten such an important piece of information? In fact, maybe I could have prevented the guy from taking us if I had thought of it. I could have told him it was in the car."

"Don't beat yourself up. You were stunned and terrified. To answer your question, no one has reported finding anything to me yet. The sheriff's department will be looking at the campsite for evidence. I've asked for their help. I'll make sure to ask about anything found in John's vehicle."

She nodded then disappeared. He stood in the middle of a brightly lit, ransacked living room holding someone else's child in his arms. He ached with the fact that he would never have this with anyone. He'd lost his chance before and didn't believe he deserved another one.

Danielle returned, holding a laptop, excitement and a measure of fear in her eyes. "I found it. I didn't know he would hide it, but he'd created a kind of hiding place for Lucy when we came to visit. It was there in the wall. And yes, sweetie, your hiding place is still there."

Reece wasn't sure if finding a hidden laptop was a good thing or not. Whoever was behind this was desperate, and desperate men were dangerous and often took crazy, illogical and unexpected risks.

At that moment, the windows suddenly shattered, underscoring his thoughts.

FOUR

Gunfire rained down on them through the windows.

Danielle reached for Lucy, who cried out, her arms outstretched for Danielle. "Mommy!"

Reece didn't release Lucy to her, but instead pulled Danielle to him. He wrapped her in his big arms. Covering both her and Lucy, Reece protected them as he rushed them behind a sofa and pushed them onto the floor. "Stay down."

He continued to cover them like he believed he was made of body armor.

"I don't understand, why is he trying to kill us?" she asked. How was she supposed to give him what he wanted if she was dead?

"We'll talk later. In the meantime, stay down. I have to get you out of here safely. I never should have brought you here."

And she never should have insisted they come here with Lucy, putting her in harm's way. Her daughter whimpered in her arms. But Danielle had thought to find what was needed to get them out of danger. Anguish gripped her heart. And Lucy's heart might not be able to take this kind of terror. She had to calm her daughter down.

"Everything will be okay, Lucy. I've got you."

"And Reece is here, Mommy. He'll protect us." Beneath Danielle, Lucy shivered.

The fact that Lucy was trying to console Danielle warmed her heart. *Oh baby.* Danielle quietly sang a Jesus song into Lucy's ear.

"Let's go." Reece motioned for Danielle and Lucy to crawl behind the sofa and then crouch.

They waited for his signal, then he covered them and rushed them to the foyer. Reece positioned them against a wall near the door.

Muscles taut and gaze intent, Reece held a gun near his chest, pointing upward toward the ceiling. He looked ready to pounce on the bad guys at any moment. The guy had been a Navy SEAL, after all. Lucy was right—Reece would protect them. He flipped the nearest light switch, turning off the living room lights, though the kitchen ones remained on. But that switch was too far.

Worry lines deepened in his forehead. Danielle had done this to him, but she was grateful that she had someone to help them, since John had been taken out of that position. She tried not to think about the fact they were in this position because of John.

"Whoever is out there is going to expect us to walk out this front door," she said.

"And we're not going to. That was never my plan. We'll stick close to the walls as we make our way around to the far side of the house, while keeping you out of the line of fire."

Reece urged Danielle and Lucy away from the foyer, sticking to the walls as they made their way around.

"Where are we going now?"

More gunfire pelted the windows, shattering more

glass. Danielle and Lucy screamed again as Reece covered them, pressing them against the floor behind a table and chairs.

"I'm going to hide you and then go take out the jerk with the gun."

"Hide us where?"

"You said your brother created a hiding place for Lucy."

"Oh yeah, right." Danielle didn't have the heart to tell him that she would never fit in there, but Lucy could.

Crawling through the house, she led him down a hallway and to an open closet. "At the back of the closet is a small door. Lucy, hon, climb into the hideaway that Uncle John made for you."

Lucy clung to her. "No, Mommy. I don't want to go in there. I'm scared. I need you."

Reece gently took Lucy. "Lucy, I need you to help me. Will you do that?"

She nodded and swiped at tears.

"I need you to help me protect you and your mom. All you have to do is climb into the hideaway. It's safe. Knowing you're safe will help me. Your mom can sit here in the closet while you're in the hiding spot. She'll be right here."

A noise in the house drew Reece's attention. "Go now. Get in."

He shut the door on them, enclosing them in darkness. Dim light still spilled from beneath the door, enough so that Danielle could assist Lucy into her hiding place. Danielle started to close the door.

"No, Mommy. Don't close the door. I'm scared."

"All right, but there might come a time when I have

to close the door to keep you safe. When that time comes, promise me you won't cry."

"I promise."

"Good, and starting now, let's be quiet, sweetie. You must help Reece, remember?"

"Okay. I won't say another word."

Danielle sat against the wall and held Lucy's outstretched hand while she sat in her little cubbyhole, hoping the moment when she would have to shut Lucy up inside would never come. Squeezing her eyes shut, she prayed, fear and panic rising in her chest, threatening to cut off her breath.

Bullets resounded. *Oh God, please keep Reece safe. Please don't let him get hurt.*

She couldn't help the tears that spilled or her shaky hand as she swiped them away. She felt completely useless in this situation.

Danielle stilled when she heard footfalls on the hardwood floor. Someone was coming down the hallway. She quietly shut Lucy up in the wall, and to her daughter's credit, she kept her promise and remained quiet.

Danielle grabbed a shoe. A shoe! That was all the protection she had. Oh wait. Danielle quietly stood and thought to pull a wire clothes hanger free, except that would definitely make too much noise, and it wasn't much protection against a gun.

The door opened, and Reece filled the space.

"Oh, Reece." She fell forward into his arms.

He held her a few moments then released her. "I shot him, but he fled. He's still out there somewhere, and you're still in danger, but for now, he's on the run."

"He got away?"

"He… It wasn't the guy who abducted you."

"Considering he gave me twenty-four hours, that would make sense, but that means someone else is after us, too." Danielle covered her face. She couldn't take this. *Oh Lord, help us!*

Reece nodded. "Let's get Lucy and leave while we still can."

"I thought I heard a siren."

"I called for backup, but I suspect neighbors probably called about the gunshots, too. Even guns with suppressors can be heard in a quiet night."

Danielle crouched and opened the door, pulling her daughter out. Fear lodged in her throat when Lucy trembled in her arms, but Lucy reached for Reece. He held her in one arm and his gun in another.

Tears blurred Danielle's vision—if Reece had even an inkling about who Lucy was, what would he do differently? But she couldn't imagine that Reece knowing the truth would change one thing in the way he cared for and protected her daughter.

The little girl trembled in his arms—she was counting on him. He wished he could snap his fingers and make it all go away. *Oh honey...*

She lifted her sweet face and looked him in the eyes. "You got this."

At the sound of her soft voice attempting to instill him with confidence, Reece's heart pinged with a powerful emotion he didn't understand, and he would need time to figure that out.

He kissed Lucy on the forehead. "Thanks for the vote of confidence. I'm going to let your mother hold you while I get us out of this, okay?"

Lucy nodded, her blond curls bouncing.

Reece released Lucy to Danielle, and the girl melted into her mother's arms. Danielle's incredibly blue eyes overflowed with gratitude. "Thank you."

"You're welcome, but honestly I wouldn't thank me just yet. We're not home free until we get you to the safe house." The place he should have taken them to begin with.

And even then, once they were at the safe house, this still wasn't over. Now there were two men involved in the race for something hidden. Something that only Danielle's brother knew about.

If only John would wake up and give them the answers.

But that was another issue. Reece focused on the here and now of their current situation at John's house.

How had Reece allowed Danielle to talk him into coming here? At least they'd found something, but even then, he wasn't sure their discovery was worth the risk to their lives. And though Reece might get them out of this mess—one he shouldn't have let them get into in the first place—he would definitely not survive unscathed. His heart's protective barrier was getting chinked with each passing hour.

He'd fallen for Danielle hard and fast when they'd been together before, and like a fool he hadn't realized just how much he loved her until he'd pushed her away and left her behind. Until it was too late. But that past they shared should have no bearing on the current predicament.

Refocusing on his task took all his power and experience. He held his weapon at the ready and carefully guided them out of the home and through the door.

Once outside, he spotted the police cruisers as they approached the house, lights flashing.

So there wouldn't be any misunderstanding, Reece put the gun away and removed his credentials then held them up high as he, Danielle and Lucy slowly exited the house.

"Special Agent Reece Bradley." He continued forward, following the sidewalk and then the driveway. Fortunately the officers didn't draw their weapons on Reece, and he'd successfully averted having them mistake him for a threat. Danielle and Lucy certainly didn't need more trauma in their night.

One of the police officers approached, and Reece acknowledged him. "Someone shot at us tonight," Reece said. "The shooter escaped and remains at large, and these two ladies aren't safe out in the open. I'll just put them in my unmarked vehicle to wait while I answer your questions."

He ushered Danielle forward to his vehicle, right by the parked cruisers with their still-flashing lights.

"Reece, what are we doing?" Lucy asked.

"Let's get you into my vehicle where you can wait and be safe and I'll talk to them, okay?"

He urged them toward the curb where he'd parked his SUV, tension rolling off him in waves. He thought he'd shot the man, but he couldn't be sure. The only thing he knew was that he'd fled the house. But he could still be out there, waiting and watching.

As Reece looked around, searching the shadows, an explosive force shook the ground and resounded in his ears.

FIVE

Danielle protected Lucy, while Reece covered them both, shielding them once again. Debris rained down on them. This time from an explosion. Had the house blown up? Had that been an accident—a gas leak? Or intentional?

And Reece's sturdy, tank-like military form protecting them from danger was turning into an unfortunate habit. Danielle fought the scream climbing up her throat as she tried to calm Lucy. Her daughter cried in her arms beneath Reece, who had pinned them down beneath him.

Her face pressed into the grass, Danielle wanted to join her and whimper and cry. Curl into herself and wait until this all went away. A million thoughts raced through her mind. Lucy's medical device, which shared vital data to the monitors via the cloud, should send out warning signals to her physicians if her heart struggled. At least Lucy's doctor would be able to see the stress they'd gone through tonight, and he would contact her if Lucy was in trouble. So Danielle shouldn't worry so much, but she couldn't help it because even if Lucy was in trouble, what could Danielle do about it at the moment? They were practically running for their lives.

Oh no, God, please help us. Then she remembered God *had* helped them. He'd sent them Reece. She had no doubt of that.

"Reece…?" Danielle tried to find the words, but her throat constricted. "What's going on?"

"It'll be okay. It's going to be okay." His confident words couldn't hide his concern. Still, Danielle couldn't remember when she had felt so safe. Even in the middle of this new terror, a sense of protection wrapped around her.

She could believe the words she told her daughter and repeated them. "It's going to be okay, Lucy. Just wait a little longer."

Tears of gratitude were still leaking from her eyes when Reece picked Lucy up and assisted Danielle to her feet. She brushed off the dirt and grass. Even managed a smile at a purple petunia that had gotten stuck in Lucy's hair. She let her gaze drift to their protector. When Reece looked at her, he seemed to focus on the tears that clung to her cheeks, and she quickly wiped them away. His face twisted up like he was in pain. He pulled his gaze away to the house in flames. Danielle hadn't wanted to look, but the crackling fire and heat compelled her to take in John's obliterated house.

Her heart palpitated, battering irregularly against her rib cage. It was too much to take in all at the same time.

"Mommy?" Lucy's voice croaked.

Danielle could feel the pain in Lucy's tone, and though Reece still held on to her, Danielle ran her hand gently down Lucy's back in reassurance.

"Baby, it's all right," she said. "We're going to find a safe place to get you snuggled into a cozy bed."

Danielle felt Reece's gaze on her. She hoped the place

he had found for them had a cozy bed. She hoped it was safe, too. She'd just have to trust him. This was all on her. She'd insisted they come to John's house. Still, they had the laptop—John's laptop that he'd hidden away in Lucy's spot for a reason.

"You okay?" Danielle asked Lucy.

Her daughter nodded, and Reece once again handed her off to Danielle. Taking her daughter from him felt so completely normal, as if she and Reece were Lucy's parents and had built the rhythm of caring for their child.

But what did that matter when all that truly counted was that they survived this? Add to that, all this shooting and bombing and running was just too much. It was too much for Danielle. And it was especially too much for her little girl. She needed her rest and to feel safe. Danielle had made a huge mistake in coming to John's house—but then again, what choice did she have if she wanted answers?

She rubbed her temples. John's house was a complete loss, so there was no point in continuing to stand here and watch.

More sirens echoed through the night. Danielle shared a look with Reece. In his eyes, she saw that he understood, maybe even shared, Danielle's feeling that it was time to get out of here. He ushered her the rest of the way to his vehicle and opened the door. They'd almost made it to the curb when the house had exploded. She slid Lucy into the back seat and used her jacket to cover her. "Lucy, I need to talk to Reece for a minute. I'll stand right here, okay? You'll be able to see me." Lucy mumbled in response, clearly exhausted as she lay down in the seat and closed her eyes.

Danielle gently shut the door and turned to Reece, who

filled her vision. Now that Lucy was resting, and Danielle didn't have to keep up the composed facade, the adrenaline suddenly rushed out of her. She trembled uncontrollably. Reece stepped forward and pulled her against him. He hugged her as if she was precious and poured strength into her. If only she could truly soak it up.

Finally she gained control and took a long breath. More emergency vehicles had arrived, including two fire trucks to put out the flames. A couple of police officers stood nearby and watched them—probably wanting to get their statements.

Reece released her and gently gripped her arms as he pinned her with his gaze. "You're done investigating. You don't know what this guy wants. Nor are you expected to find whatever it is he wanted and deliver it to these criminals. Let investigators look into this for you while you and Lucy wait somewhere safe. Are we agreed?"

Danielle had no words and simply nodded. He opened the door for her. "Get in."

"Won't I need to give my statement? And what about this?" She'd been holding on to the laptop through it all, believing it held important information. "I don't want to give it up. I want to look at what's on it first."

"Normally that would be a no, but under the circumstances, I'm not as concerned about securing evidence as I am about finding who is after you and why. I know I said to let the investigators look into this, but we'll at least check out the laptop first. You can look through it at the safe house, and then I'll hand it over to the technical gurus. As for *your* statement, I'll take that later."

"But you—"

"Relax, Danielle."

Danielle should just be quiet. She didn't understand what was going on, nor how any of this worked within law enforcement. If he was authorized to take her statement, then she wouldn't argue.

Reece gave her what he obviously meant to be a reassuring smile, and Danielle let him shut her in the car. He turned and stood between her and the police officers like a sentinel. She rested her head against the seat back and lowered the window a smidge so she could hear what was said without disturbing Lucy.

Danielle let the tension roll out of her. Reece was right—she couldn't do this to Lucy. She didn't know what the man wanted. She was relieved the burden had been removed from her. Once she and Lucy were finally at the safe house Reece had found for them, she would work from there and do what she could.

As a freelance writer, she knew her way around the internet and archives and had a few tricks up her sleeve on how to find information. She was pretty sure that's what this was all about. Information.

Deadly information.

Arms crossed, Reece informed the two officers who waited to take his statement that he would likely be working the investigation since the homeowner had been shot within the national recreation area that fell under the ISB jurisdiction. Since the home was within the city limit, he welcomed their assistance in a joint investigation if their detective wanted to give him a call. Working together, they could find the killer. Reece was all about teamwork. He had to be. They all had to be.

Since he'd been shot at and returned fire, he could potentially be put on desk duty, except he didn't have time for criminal, administrative and civil investigations. He would contact his superior about all the details and hope for the best.

The shooter was on the run. If he turned up at a hospital, they would know about it soon enough.

But this had been a different man than the one who abducted Danielle and Lucy.

Had the shooter/bomber been trying to kill *them* or kill Reece and then abduct Danielle and Lucy again? Was he working with the previous man or were they each on a race against time, seeking for themselves what John had hidden?

In that case, Danielle and Lucy were in double the danger.

He focused on answering the officers' questions and worked to keep his composure while only half his attention was on them. The other half remained wary and on edge, continually thinking through his options.

Bottom line: Whoever was after Danielle and Lucy, and even John, would keep coming back until they had what they wanted. He wished John would wake up soon so they would know what someone was after and be done with this—to a degree.

With John incapacitated in the hospital and her husband gone, Danielle was all alone in this world. Her parents had died in a car wreck a decade ago. In contrast, Reece had two brothers and a sister—a big family that was growing, with both Katelyn and Ryan getting married. And Ryan and Tori had a child on the way.

But Danielle was all alone, and Reece could do no less than stick with her through this even though he hadn't officially been assigned that task. He hoped his superior would allow him the freedom to protect her while he investigated because Reece needed to keep his badge and his gun and stay connected to those who would provide backup. It would be a balancing act, if he wanted to figure this out before it was too late.

By the time he'd finished talking with the officers, the firemen had nearly contained the house fire.

Reece marched around to the driver's side of his SUV. He stood at his door for a moment and looked inside. Danielle slept in the passenger seat and Lucy was curled in a ball in the back seat with Danielle's jacket covering her. They had both been through traumatic events today—more than anyone should have to experience. The whole day had been filled with terrifying twists and turns.

He didn't fully understand Lucy's heart condition and what this kind of day could do to her, but that was definitely a concern. He would ask Danielle about taking Lucy to a doctor for a checkup, except he had the feeling she was over-the-top protective when it came to her little girl—and if Lucy needed a doctor, Danielle was already on it. Who was he to interfere?

Warmth curled around his heart in a completely unfamiliar sensation.

When he climbed into the driver's seat, Danielle stirred, her eyes glassy. She'd been through a lot but remained strong. He reached over and grabbed her hand and was surprised at the unexpected jolt he received. That took him back to those two months with her.

He pressed down the rising emotions. "We're heading to the safe house now."

When he released her hand and grabbed the steering wheel, she shoved her long tresses back from her face. "How…how do we get there without leading whoever is after us there, too? I know you have a plan and I trust you. Maybe I've watched a few too many movies and I don't know what I'm talking about."

Reece injected a smile into his reply. "I'm glad you trust me. You get some sleep and keep on trusting me, okay?"

She nodded, and there in her eyes he saw the trust. After what happened before, how he'd simply dropped her, he wasn't sure why she would trust him at all. But maybe it was more that though she wouldn't trust him with her heart, she had no one else to trust with her and Lucy's lives—and in the end, Lucy was her priority.

He got that in a deep, unexpected way.

He started his vehicle and slowly steered around the emergency vehicles and away from the utter devastation that used to be John Steele's house. Reece made a mental note to check on the security at John's hospital room. Not wanting to add more anxiety to Danielle's plate, he would wait to make that call.

As he drove through the neighborhood, he realized that Danielle had posed a good question. How did he get them to the safe house? Safely.

Forty-five minutes later, Reece steered through the guarded entry and coded gate at a private community at the base of a foothill near Mount Shasta. He watched the gate close behind him. He hadn't seen anyone follow. As an extra precaution, he'd discarded Danielle's cell phone. He would get her a new one. He wove around the community clubhouse and golf course, through several twisting turns of the neighborhood until finally he pulled around a cul-de-sac and turned into the drive of the safe house that sat back from the road with a nice backyard up against a wooded area and creek.

He got out to open the garage door and retrieved the small remote from under a fake rock near a bush, then parked in the garage. He waited until the garage door was completely closed before shutting off the engine. Then he hopped out and assisted Danielle and Lucy. He found the key where he'd been informed it would be waiting and opened the garage entrance into the house.

"Wait here," he whispered. Though he believed the house was safe—after all, it was supposed to be a safe house—he wouldn't presume that to be truth, and he quickly cleared it, turning on lights as he went.

Once it was cleared, he made to return to the garage but found them already inside. Lucy sat on the kitchen counter rubbing her eyes. Poor girl.

"She's going to be exhausted in the morning." Danielle yawned.

"As are you. The good news is that you can both sleep in. I'll fix a late breakfast for you." He had the sudden urge to give her a peck on the cheek. To reassure her? Or something more? Whatever the reason, he felt completely responsible for protecting the both of them.

"Let's get you settled in a room, which should be easy enough. I'm told the place has five bedrooms."

"It's certainly nice." Danielle peered around the kitchen. "Fancier than any place we've ever lived. Of course, John always lived in nice houses, including the one that was destroyed, so it's not like I haven't seen luxury."

Reece grabbed Lucy from the counter. "Come on, let's find your rooms."

He led Danielle and Lucy down a long hallway. He'd been told there was also a safe room in the house, but he would need to locate and confirm it was actually safe, then he would share that news with Danielle.

He stopped at a bedroom on the right. "Lucy could sleep in here."

"Um… Tonight, at least, I want her with me. Is there another bedroom with a bigger bed, or two twins? Something?"

"I think I saw one." He led her farther down the hallway and found the room on the right. He'd left the lights on, and led Danielle and Lucy into a spacious master bedroom with a king bed. "What about this room? There's even a private bath."

Without replying, Danielle put Lucy in the big king bed and tucked her in. Or maybe that was her answer. Lucy curled into a ball again and sighed as though the day she'd experienced was like every other day. Love poured from Danielle's features as she looked at her daughter, concern in her eyes. Finally a measure of peace settled in her face, and she lifted her gaze to Reece.

He should go now. Danielle would go to bed, too. But she approached him.

Danielle stood close to him and looked up into his face. "I can't thank you enough, Reece. I can't help but think if anyone else had come to help us, we would be in an entirely different situation. Possibly dead, or still in danger, or at the very least uncomfortable."

She rose up on her toes and kissed him on the cheek.

Reece's heart stopped—or it felt that way. He hadn't taken a breath since her lips touched his cheek. He nodded then stepped back and closed the door behind him.

Then and only then could he breathe.

Oh God, help me keep them safe.

SIX

Danielle woke up with a start.

Where am I?

Chaotic memories rushed at her. She pressed her hands over her eyes. Yesterday hadn't been a dream. She slowly sat up then gasped.

Lucy! She looked to her left. Lucy had shared the king bed with her last night.

But Lucy was gone. "Lucy?"

Oh no. Danielle threw off the covers and got out of bed. She couldn't believe she'd actually fallen asleep. Or that Lucy had gotten out of bed without her noticing. What kind of mother was she?

She headed to the master bathroom and eased the door opened. "Lucy?"

Her little girl wasn't there, either. Waking up in a strange place was bad enough. Finding Lucy gone was unsettling at the very least. She pushed the panic down and exited the bathroom, opened the bedroom door and hurried down the hallway of the strange but supposedly safe home. The aromas of bacon, eggs and—was that pancakes?—wafted over her. Her stomach rumbled and her mouth watered. In the kitchen, Lucy sat on a stool at the granite counter eating pancakes slathered in syrup.

Relief whooshed through Danielle, along with un-shed tears. *Oh, Lucy.* Danielle hung her head and re-leased an incredulous laugh. She'd been worried for nothing.

"Good morning, Mommy." Lucy sounded happy and nothing at all like she hadn't slept half the night since they'd been abducted, shot at and survived an explosion.

Danielle rushed forward and gave Lucy a big hug. If it was up to her, she would hold on to her daughter forever. At least she could hold on to her until her pounding heart rate returned to normal. Danielle be-came aware that Reece watched her from the stove, where he cooked. Well, he glanced back and forth be-tween her and the bacon.

"Ouch!" He flinched when bacon grease popped.

"You'd better be careful," she said. "You want me to do it?"

"I got this."

"You didn't have to, you know?"

"I wanted to. You guys had a long, hard night and needed a hearty breakfast. Besides, I'm hungry, too."

"No, I meant, you didn't have to fry the bacon up in a pan. The oven works just as well and is less mess." She was only teasing about her intended meaning behind the words—he didn't really have to cook them break-fast, but she appreciated it.

He stared at her. "That would be way too easy."

Bacon grease popped and he flinched again, then refocused on the pan.

Danielle looked at the syrup ingredients. She didn't want to be so picky when Reece was being so good to them, but she wouldn't have fed her daughter sugary syrup. Pure maple syrup, if anything, but even then, she rarely made pancakes. Lucy needed an excellent diet to thwart off a dip in her immune system and in turn any threat of illness that could be hard on her heart.

She caught Lucy's big blue eyes observing her and making her seem wise beyond her years. Realization dawned about what day it was. Danielle blinked back the sudden surge of tears. Again. She was tired of the constant threat of tears.

She placed her palms on Lucy's cheeks. "Happy birthday, sweetie!"

Reece had plated the bacon and eggs and slid them onto the counter.

"It's your birthday?" His eyes flashed to Danielle, a measure of regret in them. "How old are you?"

She swallowed the bit of pancake she'd chewed. "I'm six years old now. My uncle John had planned a party for me. That's why we were coming out to California to see him."

Her eyes shimmered with expectation, but her mouth remained flat, as though she understood those hopes might be dashed with yesterday's turn of events.

Danielle could not take this. "I'm sorry, honey. We'll get you presents."

She'd made a mistake in letting her brother persuade her to come see him on such short notice, and look what happened.

"No, Mommy. I don't care about presents. I want Uncle John to be all right. That's more important."

"Oh, honey." Danielle hugged Lucy to her. If her intention was to keep her child happy and carefree, she was failing miserably. Anger at her brother knifed through her.

Reece stood next to her and wrapped his arms around the both of them.

Lucy started giggling, and Danielle allowed herself to join. Reece laughed, too.

They were one big happy family, and the thought stilled her heart. She moved around the counter to eat her bacon and eggs, hoping Reece wouldn't notice the shift in her demeanor.

He crouched to look Lucy in the eyes. "As soon as we can, we'll go see your uncle John. I'm praying that he gets better soon."

"You're praying, too? With the both of us praying, and Mommy, too, he has to get better."

Danielle couldn't bear to see Lucy disappointed and hoped her brother would soon come out of the coma. When she finished eating, she slid onto a stool next to Lucy and ran her hand over her daughter's hair. She glanced at Reece and caught the small smile tugging at his lips. Toys might not be at the forefront of Lucy's mind right now, but when this was all over, she would give her daughter a special birthday party and the best present ever—once she figured out what that might be.

After cleaning up the breakfast dishes, she and Lucy showered and changed into fresh clothes from the luggage Reece had thought to retrieve from her rental car. Then she settled Lucy on the sofa with a Dr. Seuss book she found on the bookshelves filled with books—classic novels for all ages. She hadn't had a chance to speak to Reece yet about the house. To whom did it belong? No family photos had been displayed on the walls, but instead the house had been decorated in soft watercolors and sketches of the coast and the mountains. Nature images meant to comfort and soothe, and the home *felt* like it had been lived in.

Reece ended a phone call and stepped back into the house from the porch, which faced a well-groomed backyard as well as a wooded area edging the yard.

"Can I look at my brother's laptop now?" she asked. "I want to get busy."

He nodded and slipped into one of the bedrooms, though she had the feeling he hadn't slept in there. He'd been prowling the house to protect them. He returned with the laptop and sat next to her as he handed it over.

"If you have a list of birthday presents, I can see about getting those. I spied a cake mix in the pantry, and I could make that for her so today is special. We can celebrate as big or as small as you want."

"Oh, Reece. Thank you for being so considerate. Lucy seems happy enough."

"Maybe we could make her the cake, give her a couple of presents and let her know we'll throw her a much bigger party when this is over."

We.

He'd said the word *we*. She hadn't even considered him being a part of their lives when this was over. His demeanor shifted slightly. Was he thinking about his words and wanting to backpedal?

She traced her finger over the laptop. "I think that sounds nice."

He tugged his cell out. "Can you think of anything we could get her for a small party tonight? Just the three of us?"

"John was supposed to buy the presents. I didn't see them in his house, but I wasn't looking for them. Obviously if they were there, they're gone now." She pressed her hands over her eyes. Her brother was in a coma, and she and Lucy were in danger and hiding in a safe house. This wasn't supposed to happen.

Lucy turned a page in her book, a slight furrow in her brow, then she looked up at Danielle as if listening in on their conversation. For her sake, Danielle had to get a grip. "Read your book, baby. Maybe we can go for a walk outside in the backyard and get some sunshine later."

She didn't even look at Reece for his reaction to that.

Lucy yawned. "Mommy, can I lie down?"

"What's the matter?" Concern inched up. "Don't you feel well?"

"I'm just tired."

"Of course you can take a nap." Dread filled Danielle. She ushered Lucy into the bedroom and tucked her in. But she should expect Lucy would be tired. Last night was harrowing. In fact, Danielle would curl up next to Lucy and nap, too, if she thought she would actually sleep, but too many things needed her attention.

If Danielle was ever concerned about Lucy's health, she would call Danielle's doctor to see what he thought about her vitals. To check if he'd looked at the data being tracked to make sure that Lucy was okay. She was probably overreacting, and if she wasn't, the doctor would call her…except she needed to replace her phone. She'd let Reece know. In the chaos, that particular detail hadn't occurred to her. She fought the need to get on a plane and fly back to Kentucky and rush Lucy to her doctor.

Danielle found Reece waiting in the kitchen, the laptop opened already. He hadn't waited for her.

She rubbed her forehead. "I think I might call Danielle's doctor. Can I borrow your cell phone?"

He flicked his eyes to her, a jolt of concern flooding his gaze. "Is something wrong?"

"Honestly, I worry over her too much, and he'll probably tell me that. But I'm cautious. I just want to make sure she is all right."

"And that's completely understandable. It can't hurt to call him and see what he thinks. Would he want you to fly back to see him?"

She shook her head. "I don't know. But I think after the last twenty-four hours, that would be too much for Lucy. It's a lot for anyone, in fact. If there was a concern, he could refer us to someone here. In the meantime, he could also call me…if he had my number."

Reece slipped from the stool and approached. He took her hands in his. "I'll get you a new cell. In the meantime, call him and give him my number. I'm here to help in any way. You have one special little girl there."

Special little girl. If only he knew…

Unable to look him in the eyes, she stared down at her hands in his.

"When you've taken care of Lucy, and your fears are dissuaded, I want to know everything about your brother."

Reece couldn't look at the laptop without Danielle. After all, she was the one who knew John and could more quickly identify any anomalies. Plus, he was concerned about Lucy, so he waited while Danielle contacted Lucy's physician in Kentucky using his cell. She ended up leaving a message for the doctor to call if he had any concerns.

When Danielle was ready to share, if she ever was, he wanted to know more about the little girl. But for now, he had to keep them safe, and that started with learning everything he could about her brother, John Steele.

John was at the center of this investigation and the reason for the danger to Danielle and Lucy.

Danielle sighed and slid onto the stool next to him. Elbows on the counter, she rested her forehead in her hands.

"Talk to me," Reece said. "What are you thinking?" *What are you feeling?*

"I'm sure Lucy is okay. The data from her pacemaker is uploaded to the cloud and monitored that way. I shouldn't worry so much. She's smiling and seems fine, and honestly, anyone would be exhausted after the day we had."

"Including you. Why don't you take a nap, too?" He resisted reaching over to squeeze her shoulder.

She lifted her head so her eyes met his. "I wish I could. But no, we need to figure this out."

She stared at the laptop, which had remained closed, but didn't make a move for it.

"Hey, it's going to be okay." He hated the meaningless phrase, but he didn't know how to encourage her.

She slowly lifted her gaze from the laptop back to him. "Is it?"

Maybe he shouldn't try to sugarcoat things, but… "I'll do everything in my power to make sure it is. That's all I can do. That includes remaining upbeat and staying encouraged—for you, and for your daughter. I know that you, as a mother, will do everything you can to take care of Lucy. If there's anything I can do to help in that department, please don't hesitate to let me know."

A tenuous smile emerged on her lips. Reece tried not to focus on those lips—but memories of past kisses surfaced. He pushed them away with thoughts of last night's gunshots and explosion.

She slowly lifted a hand and pressed it over his. He felt the soft skin of her palm. "Thank you. You've already done more than you know. Lucy is taken with you. Did you know that?" She gave a soft chuckle. "I can't deny that you've made the both of us feel safe. And you're right. We have to remain upbeat for her sake. This situation is already far too precarious, and any measure of stability we can give her will help keep her healthy."

He cleared his throat. Was there some aspect he was missing here? Would Lucy be better off in a special care facility to monitor and protect her? Maybe suggesting that would be overstepping on his part. He trusted they were not at the juncture to make such a decision yet. He realized, too, that Lucy would be at her best in every situation as long as she remained with her mother. So, it was up to him to keep them both safe, happy and healthy.

The thought, the feelings, seemed far more personal than he had a right or should even entertain.

"I'm glad we're in agreement." He offered her a smile that he did indeed feel, in spite of the circumstances.

He had the eerie sense he was part of a family. Warmth surged, but he shoved it away. He'd hurt Danielle before, and he didn't trust himself to not hurt her again. He would do the unselfish act this time. Reece would protect Danielle from all danger, and that included him. He was dangerous to her heart. He would protect her from himself even as he gave his best on this investigation.

Danielle reached for the laptop, but he stopped her. "I want to hear about your brother before we look. I want to know your thoughts before anything we might find on his laptop clouds my thinking."

Grabbing a pen from the counter, he opened his notebook.

"Is that your investigator's notebook?"

"Yep. It'll help me keep track of things." He smiled. "So relax, Danielle. Just tell me what you know about your brother. Let's stick to recent facts, say, the last few years."

"Gotcha." Elbow on the counter, she rested her chin in her hand. "I hate to say it. John and I have always been close, but we've had our own lives and have been separated by distance. So I don't know the everyday workings of his life. He divorced three years ago. I don't know why, but I suspect he put too much energy into his job and neglected his marriage. Again, I could be completely wrong about that. I think he didn't share much because we were going through everything with Lucy. Getting the pacemaker in was so traumatic. He didn't want to burden me. I know that he traveled a lot to attend conferences and award ceremonies within the industry for which he worked. He was a kind of rising star at his company to have made it to his position so quickly."

"And what is that industry?"

Her face colored. "I don't know exactly. Something

biochemistry, I think. He changed jobs a couple of times—upward mobility." She hung her head.

"It's okay, Danielle. You've had your hands busy with a beautiful little girl and her health, and also the loss of your husband. I can find his company information out somewhere else."

"No. Let me do that. I can do the easy stuff. I'm a freelance writer—newspapers, websites, magazines, you name it. I've provided for us—well, with the help of Tom's life insurance policy—but I'm good at what I do. I know how to research. I can help you. Please. I'd rather help than sit here and do nothing, especially since I'm a target."

"I don't blame you, nor do I think you should do nothing."

"Working on this will help keep me from, well, going nuts."

Reece smiled. He completely understood that thinking, and he admired her determination. "I'd love to read some of your articles. Will you share a few with me? Or send me in the right direction and I can find them myself?"

"Even better, I'll send you the link to my website."

"You have a website?" Why hadn't he even considered that and looked her up?

In response she smiled. "About John, honestly, that's all I know about my brother. Can we open the laptop now?"

Reece's cell rang, and he glanced at the call. Joel O'Reilly, his trusted ally at the state forensics lab, willing to work all hours. Perfect timing. "Sure. Go ahead. I need to take this call, but I want to look at the laptop, too, and then we need to turn it over. Please don't change anything. I'm stepping out of order on the proper chain of evidence in this case, but that's because we need some intel to keep you safe. I don't mind bending the rules in this situation." And he hoped he wouldn't be reprimanded for it.

He made his way onto the deck in the back as he answered the cell.

"We got ballistics on the bullet that killed Greg Lewis."

Greg Lewis was the murder victim found at Foreman's Creek, the case Reece was investigating when he ran into Danielle at the convenience store. "And?"

"I don't like to provide this information so soon. But since they're the same caliber, I went ahead and compared the bullets from last night's shooting to the bullet taken from Greg's body, like you requested—or rather demanded."

"How about persuaded?"

"Fair enough."

"And?" Reece held his breath.

"Using 3-D imaging technology, my preliminary findings suggest that the striations match. Right now I think there's an eighty percent chance the bullets came from the same gun."

SEVEN

Lucy woke up from her nap, so instead of perusing John's laptop, Danielle fixed Lucy a snack. She would really love to know to whom the place belonged, or was the sole purpose of this house to serve as a safe house for those in trouble? What did neighbors think about that? There was so much she didn't know or understand about this process, and she didn't like being put in the position of experiencing what it was like to stay in a safe house.

She poured Lucy almond milk and got out a fresh vegetable tray and hummus. Someone had stocked the house before they'd even arrived—with healthy fare, too (except for the pancake syrup), though there were plenty of choices, including regular milk. That meant at least one more person other than Reece knew that she and Lucy were here.

Then again, maybe the person who had stocked the fridge didn't know that Danielle and Lucy specifically were here, but simply that the house would be occupied. Danielle should just let go of all the stress. Constant worry was wreaking havoc on her nerves. Surely she didn't need to worry about this additional person.

Lucy sat at the small round table in the breakfast nook to eat her snack, and Danielle sat with her. She shoved a small golden lock behind Lucy's ear. Danielle took in her daughter's appearance and noted her skin tone looked nice and healthy. Not pale or blue. She released a slow exhale. Lucy was good, and Danielle needed to ease off the constant hovering.

She relaxed back in the chair, and through the kitchen nook window, she watched Reece on the phone, tall and handsome with broad shoulders. Why wasn't he already taken? He hadn't said that he wasn't, but she hadn't noticed a wedding ring—how ridiculous was it that she'd looked? But something about him just let her know there wasn't someone special waiting for him at home.

Or that could be her subconscious and wishful thinking.

More than that, he portrayed a protective demeanor that she couldn't ignore if she tried. She wasn't sure why she would want to ignore that, except it sent her heart back to that brief time with him. She'd sensed that same protective nature in him before, too, just beneath the surface, but then…then he'd left.

Still, he was different now. Protective and not so eager to escape…

Of course that had everything to do with his job, but she had the feeling he might be doing much more than his special agent position required of him.

Suddenly he turned away so she couldn't see him, but she heard his raised voice. She hoped Lucy didn't pay attention to the heated discussion. It might scare her. This trip and everything that had happened since they arrived in Northern California had been too much for her daughter as it was. Who was she kidding? It was too much for anyone.

She glanced at her daughter, whose big blue eyes had finally riveted to the window.

Time to redirect. Danielle pointed at Lucy's snack. "Eat up, baby. Then I'll set you up to watch television for a while. Mommy has to work. After that, maybe we can get some sunshine in the backyard."

"Is Reece mad?"

"It isn't your concern, sweetie. He has a job to do. If he needs to take a stand about something, that isn't our business."

"But we trust him to take care of us, don't we?"

Lucy's words sent a measure of fear through Danielle. Could she ever trust anyone that much? She wanted to, and at this moment she didn't have much choice. But she didn't want her baby girl getting hurt. "We trust God to take care of us, Lucy."

Lucy's smile was golden. Danielle's reply satisfied her daughter, and Lucy focused on her snack. Tucked her blond curls behind her ears. Danielle tried not to let herself worry that even though Lucy's creamy-white complexion was a healthy color, her big blue eyes were slightly bloodshot and tired. But they still sparked with life.

I need to trust You, Lord, just like I tell Lucy to trust You.

Danielle was so glad she'd found the Lord in time to give Lucy that foundation. Her little girl knew Jesus personally, and there was no greater joy for Danielle. Though she didn't understand why this was happening, she held on to her faith, and she would continue to hold on no matter what happened.

Love for Lucy, and for the Lord, surged through Danielle, and she forced back the tears. Danielle grabbed the laptop from the counter and moved it to the table so she could be next to Lucy while she finished her snack.

She opened it realizing she now had to face off with the log-in. Elbows on the counter, she rested her forehead in her hands.

"What's the matter, Mommy? Do you need a snack, too?"

"No. I need Uncle John's password to his computer." She was surprised he didn't have it set to facial recognition or some kind of biometrics, as it was. That would make more sense. Neither she nor Reece had thought that far ahead. But she wouldn't beat herself up.

"Oh, that's easy. Try Mushroomkitty24."

Danielle giggled for Lucy's sake. "You're being silly."

Lucy laughed, too. "Uncle John was only teasing me, wasn't he?"

"Teasing you about what?"

"When he asked me what his password should be. He was always teasing me."

Danielle scratched her head. Could it be? She typed in the password. The laptop processed the request, and Danielle found herself looking at the launch pad. She arched both brows and stared at Lucy. "He wasn't teasing, Lucy. He used your password." She could hardly believe it. "Can I ask you something?"

Lucy crunched on a cucumber, chewed and then swallowed as she nodded.

"Why Mushroomkitty24?"

"He was asking me about what I wanted for my birthday dinner." Her mouth drew down. "I told him I didn't care as long as it didn't have mushrooms in it. I don't like your beef stroganoff very much because of the mushrooms."

"Well, some kind of mother I am. I didn't even know that."

Lucy smiled. "It's okay, Mommy. I love you so I eat your stroganoff."

Not very much of it, though, Danielle had noted. She should have realized the reason. "Let's make a deal. Next time you don't like something, please tell me, okay?"

"You promise I won't have to eat it?"

"I can't promise that, but I'll take it into consideration. Now, why kitty?"

"He asked what I wanted for my birthday, and I told him a kitty."

Danielle had guessed that part but wanted to hear Lucy say so. Lucy had been begging Danielle for a pet—a puppy, a kitten, a lizard or a fish. Maybe that's why she hadn't seen any presents in John's home—though she hadn't been looking. Maybe John had planned to take her somewhere to pick out a kitten instead of tackling the list Danielle had sent him. Or maybe this dangerous situation had him running without another thought of Lucy's birthday. Danielle really didn't know. Her heart ached for her brother's predicament. She pushed away the rising anger—for the moment. She wanted to be in the room with him now, holding his hand, praying. Reading to him. Something. But she had to keep Lucy safe. Figuring this out would help keep John safe, too.

God, please help him get better.

Danielle focused on searching John's computer for anything that could help.

"Aren't you going to ask me about the twenty-four?" Lucy asked.

Her question drew Danielle's attention from the screen. "Oh, you're right. So why the number twenty-four?"

"Uncle John said that two plus four is six, and that would help him to remember how old I'm going to be on my birthday."

Oh, John. "He really loves you so much, Lucy."

"I know." Lucy's demeanor shifted.

Danielle left her seat to hug Lucy. "Oh, honey. It's going to be okay. He's going to be all right. We have to keep praying."

"I know, Mommy. I was thinking of how he looked in the hospital, and it made me sad. But you know what makes me happy?"

"What's that?"

"Reece. He's big and strong and handsome, and I feel safe with him."

Weird. Danielle had been thinking that exact thing only moments before. She guessed the proverbial apple didn't fall far from the tree.

"Do you think he likes kitties?"

Danielle peered into Lucy's eyes. She hated that Lucy was already growing attached to Reece. She had to protect her little girl. "I don't know, honey, but remember when this is all over, after he has protected us and everything goes back to normal, we'll go home and Reece will stay here. He's our friend and lives here. Like Uncle John lives here and you talk to him." Oops, maybe she shouldn't have added that last part.

"Are you saying that when we go home, after Uncle John gets better, that we can still talk to him but we can also keep talking to Reece?"

"Uh... I..." Danielle wasn't sure how to disentangle from this conversation.

"Mommy, are you afraid I'm going to fall in love with Reece?"

Lucy's words left her stunned. After a few heartbeats, she said, "No, honey. I know you're not going to fall in love with him. He's much too old for you, and really more like a..." Oh dear.

"More like a what, Mommy?"

"Um..."

"A daddy?"

"Maybe."

"Then are you afraid that *you're* going to fall in love with Reece?"

"Did someone mention my name?" Reece strolled in like a rushing whirlwind to suck up all the oxygen.

Reece kept his forced smile in place as he approached.

He'd had to let Danielle know that he'd come back into the house and was in the room. He'd had to interrupt her because he didn't want to hear her response to Lucy's question. Listening in wouldn't have been right to begin with, but add to that, she would have known he was there and heard the conversation. That would have made the situation awkward.

But Lucy's question had almost cemented his feet to the floor.

Danielle kissed Lucy on the forehead, then smiled up at him as she rose to stand. "Reece."

She shoved her hair behind her ears and tried to cover

that Lucy's question had left her flustered. Lucy's question and Reece's interruption. Her cheeks had flushed a pretty pink.

Oh, now Reece almost wished he would have waited for her answer, but no matter her response, he would have been distracted by it. So he'd made the right decision.

"Lucy was asking about when this is all over. I explained to her that you live here and we live back in Kentucky, and when we go home, you'll stay here." Danielle urged him over to the refrigerator. She opened the door to grab a bottled water and whispered, "I had to distract her because I thought she might get upset. We heard you outside. You had to raise your voice." Danielle offered him a bottle, then closed the refrigerator. "Is everything all right?"

Reece wanted answers yesterday instead of tomorrow. He was trying to line up protection for them here while he continued to investigate. After getting the news from the crime lab, he'd made additional calls. He peered at the opened laptop. "Everything's fine. I see you've been making progress."

"First, I had to break the code, and Lucy helped with that." She chuckled and scraped the laptop from the table to set on the counter. "Lucy, honey, you're almost finished. I want every bite gone. Reece and I are going to look at the laptop, okay?"

Reece angled it so they could both see. "I hadn't even thought about a password until I…"

Danielle's blue eyes stared up at him. Memories flooded him. He could never forget why he'd fallen in love with her to begin with. And not for the first time, he wished he hadn't walked away from her.

"Until?" Danielle waited for him to complete his sentence.

"Until I was on the phone with the computer forensics tech. I was able to get a warrant, given the fact John's in a coma and he went to the trouble to hide the laptop. They're sending someone to pick it up and also bring you a burner phone. We need to look at this fast."

"Wow, you *have* been busy today."

"Just trying to get things moving. The sooner we solve this, the better. I want you and Lucy to be safe."

"Me too. Since someone is on the way, I'm glad that John used the password that Lucy made up for him, or else I'd still be trying to get in. Can you believe it?"

"Believe what?"

"That he used her password." Danielle laughed.

"Sure I can. He adored the both of you." That's why Reece had no idea how the guy could have dragged the two of them into this, unless it all happened so fast. Came down on him. Danielle was already in the air. Already on her way there. Although, the guy could have texted they were in danger and to turn around and head home.

Then again, John might not have trusted they would be safe, even at home.

"There's something else," he said. "Deputies didn't recover anything in John's vehicle except his briefcase with a few AlphaGentronics company brochures. So I'm thinking whoever took you and Lucy also got his hands on whatever John had been going to show you. Whatever it was hasn't stopped them for looking for something more."

Danielle narrowed her eyes as if in thought. "I keep thinking that maybe whatever John was going to show me was also what he was going to give me, and somehow everything got lost in translation, and with the gunshots."

Reece shook his head in frustration. "I just wish John hadn't involved you. My two cents—and maybe I shouldn't say so—he should never have invited you here and should have told you to stay away."

He hung his head, wishing he had kept all of it to himself, but there was much more. Reece clamped down on the rest. His take was that John had been camping as a means of hiding from whomever was after him, and he knew full well the danger when he persuaded Danielle to bring Lucy to the campsite. "It's one thing to use Lucy's creative passwords, but quite another to…" He'd said too much.

When he dared lift his head to look at Danielle, she was staring at Lucy.

A small gasp escaped her lips. "You don't think…"

Danielle didn't need to finish the sentence for him to know. Had John shared what the gunman wanted with Lucy? "I don't think that Lucy is keeping a secret for John. That would be…"

"Unforgivable." Unshed tears surged in Danielle's eyes. She scraped them away. "Let's get busy."

Her hands hovered over the keyboard. "I'm not even sure where to look first."

"Is this his work laptop or his personal laptop? That's my first question."

Danielle opened up the folders. "Looks like it's personal, considering the photographs, plus personal finances. A few computer games. Legal documents. I feel like I'm intruding on his privacy."

Reece watched as Danielle pushed beyond her concern and opened file after file. She quickly scanned through the documents in the same way as he would do, though he wasn't a computer forensics expert.

"I don't know what I'm looking for, exactly," she said.

"We'll both scan at the same time, watching for anything that catches our attention."

Danielle started reading a document out loud. "AlphaGentronics Annual Reports."

She glanced up at Reece. "This…seems out of place to me."

Reece pressed fingers over his mouth in thought. "So, it stands to reason that whatever he meant to give you has to do with his work. Has to do with AlphaGentronics." Reece pressed the rising anger down. Danielle didn't need to see his growing animosity toward her brother.

The doorbell rang.

Muscles tensing, Reece shared a look with Danielle. "I'll get it."

"Mommy?" Lucy ran to her.

He hated how they were living in such fear that even an everyday sound had frightened them. "Take her to the bedroom."

Danielle reached for John's laptop, too.

"No. I'm guessing they're here for the laptop."

Danielle grabbed it anyway. "No. I need more time."

He gently took it from her. "I promise, this guy is going to find out more than we ever could. We skimmed through it hoping that something would snag your attention. Now it's time to let the experts have a go."

Reece worked to convince her, though he hadn't been

happy with the decision, either. He thought they would have more time. "Please go with Lucy. Just in case."

He brandished his weapon and then peered out the window. Anthony Hammer, the Maynor County Sheriff's Department computer forensics tech he'd secured through his detective brother, Ryan, had been willing to pick the laptop up. Reece had had to work up a network of local resources throughout his multistate region, but he had the best connections in Northern California, where he had law enforcement family.

Reece stepped onto the porch. "I'll save you some time and give you the password."

Anthony's eyes widened when he heard the password.

"Lucy came up with it for her uncle." Reece handed the laptop off. "No one followed you here, did they?"

Anthony handed Reece a sack. "No. Nobody even knows we've talked or that I was coming here. I'll give it a look. That's the burner cell you requested."

"Thanks for that. I owe you," Reece said. "John Steele works for AlphaGentronics. He has both work and personal documents on this device."

Anthony folded the laptop under his arm.

"I'm counting on you to find the answers that could save Danielle and Lucy's lives. Or at least free them from the imminent threat."

Anthony thrust out his hand. "I won't let you down."

Reece shook it. "Text me anything, big or small, that you find interesting."

"Could you give me a hint? What are you thinking this is about?" Anthony asked.

"I don't have a clue." He wanted Anthony's processes

to be free of Reece's influence. "Even if I did, I wouldn't want to sway your thinking."

"I hear you." Anthony turned and headed to his red sedan parked in the drive.

Once Reece knew more about the murder victim who had most likely been killed by the same shooter, he could formulate a theory, although he was already mulling over a few ideas and possible connections. Crossing his arms, he watched Anthony drive around the cul-de-sac and head down the street toward the gate. No other vehicles sat along the curb, waiting to follow. Or waiting to ambush them in this safe house.

Reece entered the house and locked the door behind him, set the alarms, then went in search of Danielle and Lucy. Lucy was curled up next to Danielle on the bed watching a television show. Danielle held her tablet, and her gaze lifted to him when he stood in the doorway. She disentangled herself from Lucy, who looked about ready to fall asleep again. Hadn't she just had a nap?

Danielle turned the sound down to barely discernible and closed the door but left it cracked.

Reece's throat tightened with concern for the child. But he wouldn't voice his concern and add more to Danielle's. He followed her into the kitchen.

She angled her tablet for him to see. "The company John worked for, AlphaGentronics, manufactures the medical device, the pacemaker, implanted in Lucy for her heart."

EIGHT

The way Reece stared at her, she read the question in his eyes easily enough—*you didn't know your brother's company manufactured your daughter's pacemaker?*

Okay, so yeah, she felt like an idiot. Research and knowledge was her thing—and she didn't know this small, important detail.

"Um… I don't know why I didn't realize that before." She pressed a hand to her cheek. "I would think that John knew it."

"You probably had so much on your mind. You were worried about Lucy, and the last thing you were thinking about is what company made the device. And honestly, it doesn't even matter."

"I should have guessed it was his company."

"Why should you have guessed?" He took the tablet from her and set it on the counter, then turned her to face him. Reece gently held her arms. "You're overthinking this. Listen, we don't have a lot of time to figure out what someone wants from John. What they now want from you."

She bobbed her chin. "I was far removed from California and John at the time. My husband, Tom, and John didn't get along."

She couldn't look into Reece's intense forest green eyes. Now that she thought about it, John had never liked Reece, either, and he had urged her to move on. Of course, any brother would be angry at a man who had left his sister the way Reece had left—and of course, he hadn't known that he'd left her in such a delicate way. She hadn't known, either, until a month later.

Danielle moved to the window to stare out. Reece might want to know what she was thinking, and she couldn't hide the emotions clamoring to the surface. She blinked back the tears.

She hadn't known when he left that she was pregnant with his child. She'd made a mistake when she'd allowed herself to fall for Reece—he was the wrong guy, and she knew it. He'd repeatedly told her he was leaving. He was a Navy SEAL, after all, and he'd told her that waiting on him was no life for her. Still, she thought that maybe he'd fallen in love with her a little, too. Even though she'd known he wasn't the right guy, she hadn't been able to stop her heart. She'd known he wasn't ready for commitment, and he'd been right—what kind of life would that have been for her to wait around on a guy who was always gone? No life at all, though she was older and wiser now and knew plenty of spouses waited for loved ones in jobs that took them away.

When she'd learned she was pregnant, she'd anguished over that fact at first, but she never spent even one moment regretting the child growing in her. How could she?

Tears surged in her eyes, and she carefully swiped them away, hoping he wouldn't notice. She had no idea what he was doing behind her. She hoped he was distracted.

She thought back to that time—Danielle had tried

to reach Reece, but he was on some sort of covert mission. She found herself doing exactly what he warned her he didn't want her doing—waiting on him. Then John had convinced her it was in no one's best interest to raise her child on her own. Danielle resisted at first—after all, people raised children alone all the time. But she wanted the best for Lucy. She started attending a church, and that's where she met the Lord and became a Christian. She was sure that God had brought Tom into her life then. She'd reconnected with him, a childhood sweetheart—Tom had apparently never gotten over her and was anxious to love her, make her his wife and raise Lucy as his own child. He was Lucy's father.

Oh, Tom.

Danielle released a ragged sigh.

God, please let Reese not pay any attention to me. I just can't face telling him the truth now.

Tom had married Danielle near the end of her pregnancy, and together they had made a good life for Lucy. Danielle couldn't have been happier. Though she'd conceived Lucy out of wedlock, Danielle would never think of her daughter as a mistake. Lucy was a beautiful, wonderful child for whom God had plans.

After Tom died, John kept trying to get Danielle and Lucy to move back to Northern California from Kentucky, where Tom had moved them for his job. But she hadn't wanted the reminders of her life here—case in point, Reece Bradley.

And yet here she stood in a house in California with none other than Reece Bradley, the man from her past, and… Lucy's father. Danielle reminded herself that she and Lucy had already been through so much pain. Reece had hurt Danielle by leaving her, and then Tom had hurt both her and Lucy by leaving them when he'd died. She didn't think their broken hearts could take more of that kind of pain, so she had to protect them from getting too close to Reece—at least emotionally.

"Okay, Danielle." Reece's tone was gentle and understanding. "Please tell me what's going on. What has gotten you so upset? I mean, other than the obvious precarious situation we're in."

With her back to him, Danielle shuddered.

She could feel him standing behind her. He was much too close. Danielle held her breath. She didn't want him to know she was crying. She should make an excuse and head to the bathroom to wash her face, but she feared even that small action would give her away. Before she could move, Reece rested his hands on her shoulders. A gentle and compassionate action on his part that pinged around in her heart.

"It's going to be okay. You and Lucy are safe now, and we're going to figure this out together."

"It's not going to be okay, Reece. Nothing will ever be the same." Reece had no idea what he was saying to her, nor did she have the courage to tell him any of it.

Danielle fled the room.

Reece watched Danielle rush away from him and down the hallway and into the guest bathroom. He felt helpless. What could he do?

He scraped a hand through his hair. This situation was bad enough without him feeling completely inadequate to keep Danielle encouraged and upbeat. Maybe he was only fooling himself and encouraging Danielle was a lost cause.

And this was definitely above his pay grade. No one

was asking him to reassure her and protect her while he investigated.

Reece had never been the kind of guy to give up, and he knew in his bones he was doing the right thing. He wasn't sure that his efforts mattered—he only knew that he couldn't stand to see her like this. And he didn't understand why she'd suddenly gotten upset.

Maybe memories about her deceased husband flooded her—they'd been talking about him when she'd commented that Tom and John hadn't gotten along.

The next thing he knew, she was crying. He'd left her alone with her thoughts. Who was he to intrude? But enough was enough. He'd seen her shudder, and he'd needed to comfort her.

Only his touch hadn't comforted her. Instead she'd rushed away from him. What did that mean? He should just keep his distance and give her space.

His cell buzzed with a text. Reece glanced at it. Good news, but then again, bad timing.

A soft sniffle let him know that Danielle had come out of the bathroom. Her face paled as she slowly approached. When she stood a few feet away, her features twisted in anguish and regret.

"Reece, I'm so sorry. Never mind me. This whole thing has overwhelmed me. I don't mean to have a meltdown right in front of you."

He smiled and met her halfway, taking her hands in his. "You're entitled to have all the meltdowns that you need to have. This situation is intolerable. I've been so impressed with how strong you are, Danielle. Of course, I've always known you were strong." Maybe he shouldn't have said that last part.

Danielle stepped back, a slight frown between her

brows, and then her face relaxed. "I'm strong for Lucy, Reese. Keeping her safe and well is my priority."

"It's mine, too. Are you going to be okay?" What a dumb question.

"Sure." She swiped at her eyes again. "I need to start thinking about dinner, and also baking the birthday cake. After this I'll give her a real party, but for today she can at least have the cake."

"I don't want you to have to worry about cooking or doing anything at all. I got this."

"Reece, cooking and baking will take my mind off things. Any measure of normalcy will help me to keep my head on straight. Now, I'm going to look in the freezer and see if that's as stocked as the fridge. Whose place is this, anyway? There are no family photos anywhere, so I'm left to wonder."

"I'm not at liberty to say."

She shrugged. "Well, that makes sense. Keeping everything secret protects people in these kinds of situations."

"Exactly," he said.

A knock came at the door.

Danielle tensed, a question in her eyes. Reece nodded, his confirmation that she should go check on Lucy. He peered out the window and spotted two deputies at the door. He'd been expecting them.

Reece opened the door and urged them inside.

"I'm Deputy Dale Wells." The stocky guy shook Reece's hands.

"Clay Hutchins." The tall and lean deputy fisted his hands on his hips.

"Thanks for coming out for a few hours of protection duty." Reece took in their attire. "You came in plain clothes, so that's good."

"We were told not to draw attention to this house."

"Thanks for complying. How about one of you hang around inside the house, and the other outside. Will that work?"

"If one of us is lurking outside for no reason, that can draw attention," Dale said. "It's not like I can stand outside and water the grass."

"You could, actually. But you could also lean against the vehicle and talk on your cell. Check the perimeter now and then, walking around and talking on your cell. That will look normal. Think of it as undercover work."

Clay scratched his jaw. "Are you sure it's not better to just wear our uniforms and thwart any attempts to get to them?"

"I don't want to signal this is a safe house and that targets are inside." Reese had wanted to explain to Danielle before they'd shown up, but he hadn't had the chance. "Come on in and wait in the kitchen while I go tell Danielle you're here."

He made his way down the hallway and softly knocked on the bedroom door. Lucy opened it with a smile and a hug for him. He couldn't fathom, much less explain, the joy that surged in his heart. He lifted her in his arms and entered the room, closing the door behind him. Danielle was straightening the bed where Lucy had been watching television and drifted to sleep again.

She finished and looked up. "Who was it?"

"Two deputies. I had wanted to tell you before but didn't get the chance. I have to follow up on a lead. And yes, before you ask, it involves this case." He could grab some presents, too, if Danielle would give him a list.

"But who is going to protect us?" Lucy asked.

"Deputy Wells and Deputy Hutchins."

Her eyes grew wide. "Wow, two deputies? Can I meet them?"

He chuckled and glanced at Danielle, whose reaction did not reflect Lucy's. "I'll introduce you."

Danielle hugged herself. "I don't like this."

"It's only for a little while."

"Should I plan for five for dinner?"

"I hope to be back by dinnertime and they can be on their way, so no, you don't have to. You don't even have to cook. I can bring takeout." *And a cake*, he mouthed, hoping Lucy wouldn't see.

"I told you I need the distraction. So I'm cooking."

"That's totally fine. I'm sure it will be delicious." It sounded like they were a family, and he was coming home for dinner like a father and a husband. Awkwardness rolled over him. "Come on, let's go meet the deputies. Now, Lucy, they aren't dressed like deputies."

Danielle followed him down the hallway.

"I didn't want them to draw attention to the house," he said. "They're just two friends who are visiting, okay?"

Danielle grabbed his arm and held him back. "Be careful out there, Reese. I don't want you to get hurt. I trust *you* to keep us safe. Maybe I shouldn't."

"There's something I need to show you." Reese paused at a door in the hallway. He'd hoped it wouldn't come to this. He opened the door, stepped inside and flipped on the lights. "This is the safe room."

"Wait. A safe *room*? Aren't we in a safe *house*?"

"Yes, but…worst case…" He didn't want to say more in front of Lucy.

Danielle frowned.

"The door is galvanized steel, not wood. Over there on the desk is a charging cell phone. A shotgun is in the gun safe, and the ammunition is on the shelf."

She pressed her hand over his arm to stop him from showing her. He read the message in her eyes—*not in front of Lucy*. He understood. At least Danielle knew she had a safe room inside a safe house.

"And I got you a burner cell. It's on the kitchen counter for you."

"Thank you, Reece. You've thought of everything."

He hoped.

"We have a safe house and a safe room, but what about you when you leave here?" Though a grin hitched in her lovely cheeks, he understood the seriousness of her question and the concern in her eyes.

"I promise I won't get hurt. I'm not likely to face danger with what I'm doing."

Her earlier words—about keeping them safe—could hurt him, and he was obviously more invested in the two of them—more personally invested, that was— than he should be when working this case. At the same time, he sensed something more than simple trust in her words. He reminded himself that he'd hurt her before when he'd left. He had hurt them both. And maybe her trust in him—the trust that went deeper than a victim trusting an officer of the law—was misplaced, and he needed to set her straight.

There was so much he wanted to tell her about his regrets, about his time spent in a hospital in Germany and dreaming about her. But sharing that wouldn't do either of them any good.

NINE

Reece hated leaving Danielle and Lucy behind, but then again, putting some space and distance between them was probably the best thing to clear his mind… and his heart. The two of them were at a safe house and were in good hands.

He would look into a few things and get back as soon as he could. He'd filled out the appropriate reports and been in contact with his superior. His investigations into matters involving the National Park Service included a wide array of criminal activity, but especially murder. He worked with many agencies, especially the park rangers. The investigations usually took weeks if not months, but he hoped this particular case would be solved soon, and the only way to make that happen was to get out there and investigate. He'd done all he could do from the safe house, and now it was time to get in the field and get his hands dirty.

Reece drove across town into a posh neighborhood to talk to John's ex-wife. He knocked on her door. She was slow to open, and her red-rimmed eyes grew wide when he introduced himself. Was she grieving over John's hospitalization?

"Mind if I ask you a few questions? I'm trying to get to the bottom of what happened to your ex-husband."

"No, I don't mind. Please come in." She ushered him into a spacious home. "Can I get you something to drink?"

"Thank you, but no. I don't want to take up too much of your time. I need to ask if you have any idea who might want to harm your ex-husband."

"None. John was well liked. He didn't have enemies. He was…is very intense, and he traveled, focused on his job. Things couldn't work out for us. As for enemies, he didn't have any, as far as I know."

Reece nodded. This was as he expected, but he'd had to talk to someone who knew John, and maybe knew more details of his life than Danielle.

Next up, he headed to the biotech company where John worked and sat in the parking lot waiting for a local city detective, who was teaming up with him to investigate the bombing of John's house. Reece could use the help as he focused on John's shooting and the murder in the national park.

While he waited, he read through phone records he'd downloaded to his iPad from the murdered man's cell.

One of the numbers appeared vaguely familiar. *Wait a minute…* Reece skimmed through his investigations notebook. John Steele and Greg Lewis had shared conversations. Lewis worked for a software company in San Francisco. What was their connection?

More and more, Reece was beginning to think this had everything to do with the company for which John worked. He stared up at the modern four-story complex that looked like he would imagine a biotech company would look. Sterile and polished.

A vehicle pulled into the parking spot next to him. Detective Shirley Crowder.

Reece got out of his vehicle and greeted the tall brunette detective. They headed for the doors to John's company. "I'll let you ask the questions, Detective, while I observe."

"Sounds good to me."

At the reception area, the detective flashed her credentials and introduced Reece to the male receptionist who had a crisp no-nonsense haircut to go with his demeanor.

"If you'll wait over there for a moment, I'll call someone to meet you."

Detective Crowder sat, and Reece paced the space. He couldn't shake the bad feeling crawling all over him.

Tap, tap, tap, tap... The sound of high heels clicking across the floor drew his attention. A trim redhead dressed in a professional suit and skirt headed directly for them. Detective Crowder stood and waited for her approach.

"Welcome to AlphaGentronics. My name is Cindy." Her professional smile didn't give any hint at her true thoughts. "I'm afraid our facilities are highly sensitive."

Detective Crowder nodded but said nothing.

Good.

Cindy appeared uncomfortable and her lips twitched. "What I'm saying, Detective and Special Agent, is that we'll need a warrant."

"I'm just here to ask questions," Crowder said.

"I'm afraid I can't help you without a warrant," Cindy said. "Now, if you'll excuse me."

Reece followed Crowder out into the parking lot.

Neither of them said a word until they reached their vehicles.

She tapped on her tablet. Reece waited for her to speak.

"I can't say I was expecting the cold shoulder," she said. "I would think they would want us to find out who shot their employee."

"Apparently their highly sensitive facility has things to hide," Reece said. "And maybe John was about to share some of that information, and that got him shot."

The detective smiled. "You and I are thinking along the same lines."

"You think it's enough to get a warrant?"

The detective shrugged. "We'll see what a judge thinks. I'll call you if I learn anything more. Do you have anything to add?"

He thought for a moment, then said, "John was shot and Greg Lewis was murdered—both incidents occurring in the national park." Had Greg met with John at his campsite and somehow ended up running for his life, getting lost in those woods until he was killed? Or had he planned to meet someone and that meeting had gone the wrong way?

"You're saying they could be connected?"

"I am, and they are. Cell phone records indicated they were communicating."

"But what's the connection? Why were they both shot?"

Reece wanted to head to San Francisco to look around the software firm, but he wouldn't leave Danielle. "Greg Lewis was a software guy. John Steele is a biotech guy."

Crowder crossed her arms and leaned against her

vehicle. "Corporate espionage? Hacking? Embezzlement?" She crooked a smile. "Is that even in your jurisdiction?"

"Yes." He opened his vehicle door. He'd been gone longer than he had planned. "If you get the warrant, let me know. I want to be there, if possible."

"What's your hurry? You wanna go grab a cup of coffee or something? Dinner maybe?" She offered a shrug and half a grin.

"I have somewhere I need to be. Maybe another time."

"Sure, okay. I'll let you know if I learn anything."

Reece got into his vehicle and started it. Danielle would be cooking dinner, and he didn't want to miss that. He would swing by a big box store on the way back and see if he could get a few of the items she'd texted him for Lucy's birthday. He wished they could celebrate under much different circumstances, but the sweet little girl deserved at least a cake and a few gifts on her birthday. Though he shouldn't, he realized he enjoyed that feeling of going home to family a little too much. Danielle and Lucy weren't his family. He didn't deserve them.

But he would keep them safe.

And then he would leave them... A déjà vu sensation washed over him.

Danielle had thrown together a lasagna while Reece was gone. The aroma filled the home. The birthday cake made from the yellow cake mix he'd spotted in the pantry, along with strawberry icing, was cooling on the counter.

She had fixed her hair and makeup, and now gently combed Lucy's soft hair, careful to allow the curls to have their own way. Her daughter was like a porcelain doll—beautiful and delicate. She deserved so much better than this. Danielle could almost imagine herself standing outside her body, either dreaming or watching an action movie on television. This could not be her life right now.

And yet, it was. But in this precious moment in time, she would focus back on her wonderful gift from God.

"I want my hair to be pretty like yours for Reece, Mommy. Is that why you want your hair to be pretty?"

A half smile cracked Danielle's lips. She couldn't disappoint her daughter with the negative response that filled her head, because the negative response—though a more appropriate one—would also be a lie.

What was wrong with her?

Why did being with him stir such strong emotions? Such intense longing? She couldn't stop the flood of memories of their time together, and all those memories—even the stressful, brutal memories of Reece leaving, of her learning she was pregnant—couldn't erase the quiver in her belly.

Her breathing quickened at the thought—she could not allow herself or Lucy to be hurt again. Losing Tom had almost broken them both. Reece was just the kind of person to hurt them. He'd done it before, and Danielle couldn't risk that again, especially since Lucy was now in the picture. Intense pain pinged through Danielle's chest at the thought of Lucy being hurt by Reece.

But for this moment in time, they needed this distraction…and protection.

As Reece mentioned, this was an intolerable situation, and yes, Danielle had turned to playing house. The facade kept her little girl distracted and happy.

And maybe, sure, happier than she'd ever seen Lucy since her father had died. *Her father...*

What should I do, Lord?

"Mommy? Is that why you want to be pretty?" Lucy's question drew Danielle back to the present. She took a deep breath and exhaled slowly.

Yes, Lucy...for Reece. But she couldn't admit that to Lucy. "I want my hair to look nice. But no way can it ever match up to your beautiful curls." She tickled Lucy and elicited the giggles she'd wanted.

In the meantime, she would pretend everything was okay for at least today while she put the past out of her mind. The past that had created the future, and this moment. The past that had created Lucy.

Danielle worked to tie the wide purple ribbon in her daughter's hair.

Telling Reece the truth about Lucy could trigger a mountain of grief, and she was working overtime as it was to keep Lucy happy.

And healthy.

She glanced up at the mirror. Lucy definitely looked better. More color in her cheeks. A twinkle in her blue eyes. Danielle couldn't help but think that Reece had done that for Lucy. If they were in this alone—no Reece—Lucy would be suffering. The downside, of course, was that Lucy was growing more attached to the man by the hour. Maybe even the minute.

Why shouldn't she? He'd stepped in to protect her and play a father's role.

That was, until the investigation was over.

Until they were safe again.

A sound drew her attention. Sent a tendril of fear crawling through her.

Lucy played with the lipstick Danielle had left on the counter and hadn't seemed to notice the sound. Maybe Danielle had imagined it.

Two deputies were there to protect them.

Still… "Sweetie. Stay here. I need to check on the lasagna. Work with your ribbon and get it the way you want it."

"Can I put some of your makeup on?"

Danielle sighed. She'd have to wash Lucy's face, but if it kept her occupied, then so be it. "Okay. But not too much."

"I won't. I promise. I'll put a little on, just like you, Mommy. I want to be pretty like you."

Danielle gave Lucy a smile. How could she not? While Lucy remained focused on the makeup counter, Danielle slipped away and closed the bathroom door, then the bedroom door. Slowly. Quietly.

She crept down the hallway then paused. An eerie quiet filled the home, but it was much more than that. A sensation crawled over her as if danger lurked in the home.

She was alone.

How could that be?

Two deputies were watching over them. This was a safe house. No one knew about it. Danielle continued slowly down the hallway, passing the safe room, passing the opening to the living area. A glorious bright day shined through the windows, and green leaves fluttered in a soft breeze, all of it belying the unwelcome sensation.

"Deputy Dale?"

No response. He hadn't heard her? Or…something else?

The aroma of lasagna filled the house but couldn't chase away her growing panic.

She continued toward the kitchen. Everything was okay. She was just being paranoid.

A glance in the oven at the lasagna told her it was cooking nicely and still had a few minutes to go. Then she would put the rest of the mozzarella cheese on top and put it back in for a few minutes. Looking at the lasagna didn't chase away that bad feeling. She hugged herself.

"Deputy Dale?"

He still hadn't answered. Maybe he was outside talking with the other deputy. That had to be it and she was panicking for nothing. Danielle peered out the window in the kitchen. She couldn't see either deputy. Moving across the room in the breakfast nook, she glanced out those windows, which offered a view of both the back and the side of the house.

Where had the deputies protecting her and Lucy gone? Her breathing quickened.

She should go outside and check on them, but…if something was wrong, and they were in danger—like her instincts kept telling her—then Danielle should stay inside with Lucy.

If something was wrong, then calling out the deputy's name might very well have been a mistake. Still, she wouldn't cower in the bedroom and wait for help to arrive. Danielle picked up a rolling pin. She crept through the house, her breaths coming much too quickly.

She hoped and prayed that any minute, one or both deputies would stroll into the house, laughing and joking and asking about the lasagna. She'd made that for

Reece and had assumed the two law enforcement officers would be relieved of safe house duty by dinnertime. But of course there was plenty, and she would offer it to them.

If they would only come inside from wherever they were hiding.

Across the living room, in the den, she caught sight of two shoes...attached to legs sprawled on the floor. Her pulse skyrocketed, filling her ears with the sound of her rushing blood. The deputy was on the floor, but she couldn't see all of him.

Dead? Alive? Unconscious? She wanted to rush to him, but remained frozen in place.

She held back the scream that wanted to erupt in her throat.

Goose bumps crawled over her.

Lucy...

Heart pounding, Danielle tried to slow her breaths. Heavy, loud breathing would give her away.

She was probably already found out.

And Lucy... Someone could have gotten to her already.

Danielle rushed down the hallway, passing the safe room again.

Please, God, let her be safe. Keep her safe.

She and Lucy would need to get to the safe room. The steel door. And the shotgun. There she could call for help and, worst case, use the weapon kept in the room for their protection.

Oh God... Please help us. How could it have come to this?

She rushed to the bedroom. Entered and shut the door

quietly behind her. In the bathroom she found Lucy dancing around.

She snatched her child up in her arms, pressed Lucy's face against her shoulder and whispered in her ear, "Be very, very quiet."

"Mommy?"

"Shh. No more words," she whispered. "Trust me."

Lucy shuddered. Fear could do her in, just like it threatened to take Danielle down, except Lucy was fragile. Much more fragile. Danielle crept to the bedroom door and cracked it open. Peered down the hallway.

The safe room was five yards away.

The longest distance of her life.

A shadow crossed the kitchen floor. Danielle thought her heart would stop. With a deputy down, she knew the person in the house was only there to harm them. He was closer to the safe room than she was, and she wasn't sure she could make it to that safe room. In fact, this bathroom in the bedroom might have to be their safe room.

What about the deputy outside? Deputy Clay? If the guy had made it inside the house, Deputy Clay outside was probably incapacitated, too. *Oh God, please let them not be dead.*

Danielle reached for the cell in her pocket.

Except it wasn't there. She'd left it charging in the kitchen after she'd called the doctor again to leave her new temporary number. Idiot.

That's why the safe room was…safe. The cell phone was always there charging. What a brilliant idea. And completely useless to her now if she didn't get to that room.

Clutching Lucy close to her, she peered out the smallest of cracks in the door.

The man entered the hallway. With his big strides, he would be on them in seconds.

No way would she make it. She couldn't risk that with Lucy. They were trapped.

TEN

Fear snaked around her chest and squeezed. She couldn't breathe.

Lucy. I have to save Lucy.

God, help me save Lucy!

Danielle pushed past the fear that could paralyze her. Was paralyzing her. She forced her feet to move. Locked the door—it wouldn't prevent him from coming in, but it could slow him down. She turned around in the room looking for a way to protect Lucy.

There was nothing for it. She had to escape the house. Danielle hurried to the window, still holding Lucy. In her arms her little girl trembled with fear. Why was this happening?

Oh, Reece, where are you?

The smoke alarm reverberated. Of course, the lasagna was burning. She almost laughed at how ludicrous it was to care about the lasagna right now.

The window wouldn't budge.

The doorknob twisted. He would soon kick the door down.

"Here, hide in the closet and don't come out."

Lucy whimpered and reached up.

For the first time in her life, Danielle ignored her

daughter. There was no time to comfort her if she was going to save her.

Danielle lifted the flat-screen television. It was heavy, but she had to do this. She pressed against the wall next to the door, her heart jackhammering.

The door burst open. The predator had kicked it in like she expected. He aimed his gun.

Lucy burst from the closet.

"No!" Danielle screamed at the same moment she slammed the widescreen television into the man—catching his face and his arm. The gun fired into the floor. He cried out in pain as he dropped. Danielle tried to get past the man, who was now in her way along with the broken television. It hadn't knocked him out, though, and he groaned. The gun. She could get the gun. But it was too near his hand. She couldn't risk it. He was about to stir completely and could grab her.

Lucy had collapsed in fear. Danielle thought she might collapse right next to her. But she had to stay strong. She scooped up her daughter and ran from the room and just kept running down the hallway, past the safe room. In the kitchen, she grabbed her cell phone, yanking it from the charger, and headed for the front door, then hesitated.

What if he hadn't come alone?

She took a few steps back and then headed for the back door instead of the safe room. She couldn't stay in this house one more second.

Carefully she stepped outside. Seeing no one, she sprinted across the backyard. Dense trees surrounded the creek that ran behind the house. Danielle hurried into the shadows. She whispered reassurances to Lucy and called 9-1-1. Then she called Reece and left a voice mail. But Danielle couldn't wait for help to arrive.

As Reece had told her, twenty seconds was a long time when someone was intent on harming you. The man could have composed himself by now and would come for them. She stepped into the small creek and walked over pebbles and rocks, then she stepped along the side and hopped on the small boulders. Their progress was much too slow.

Maybe Danielle should run to a neighbor's house—but the homes could be empty at this hour until people arrived home from work. She wouldn't risk pounding on a door and asking for help if nobody was even home.

"Mommy, can we stop now?"

"Oh no, baby, we have to keep going."

"For how long? I'm tired."

"You're not the one doing all the work, Lucy," Danielle teased in a light tone.

"I'm tired of you holding me."

She didn't think Lucy could maneuver the terrain as quickly as Danielle, and even she wasn't making that much progress. Was it okay to stop and rest? She lowered Lucy but held a tight grip on her hand. "Okay, let's rest by this tree." Danielle hunkered down against the tree trunk and closed her eyes. Let her breathing calm. Except that wasn't going to happen. Danielle sat in the grass next to a cedar tree. The needles hung down, and Lucy played with the fronds. If only their lives could be that simple, but this wasn't their current reality.

And in fact, this was a mistake. Every nerve ending in her body told her to keep moving.

Reece pressed the accelerator.

He'd missed a call from Danielle, but listened to the

voice mail telling him she was in trouble. On his cell he contacted the local dispatch. Units were on the way.

His earlier conversation about the seconds it took for a criminal to do harm swarmed through his insides now.

Oh God, please keep them safe.

His heart ached as panic spread through his chest. He swerved in and out of traffic while trying to contact the two deputies he'd left at the safe house to protect Danielle and Lucy. Their lack of response painted horrific images in his mind.

Reece texted her that he was on his way. He wouldn't try to call Danielle back, because she could be in a precarious position if she was hiding. The last thing she needed was for her cell to go off. He hoped that even a text wouldn't cause harm to her. He would trust her to call him back. He swerved around a corner and saw the cul-de-sac at the end of the street.

The house was in sight. He waited patiently for the gate to open then he turned onto the street and steered right into the yard. Behind him two cruisers—sirens blaring—pulled in. He'd beaten them here.

His heart sank. He would have preferred they were already here.

Please be okay. Please be okay.

Reece quickly flashed his credentials as he moved toward the house, so the new deputies would know he was law enforcement. "I called for an ambulance, too," he said.

With the words, an ambulance pulled up. Reece crouched and felt for a pulse on Clay. Still alive. *Thank You, Lord!*

"I don't see a wound on him," Reece said.

The officer crouched, too. "Could have been knocked unconscious."

A couple of medics ran up to the downed deputy, and Reece left Clay in good hands.

Two officers had already approached the door.

Reece joined them. "A woman and child could be inside. Someone is trying to kill them."

Or they could already have been taken. Or…worse. Killed. Reece couldn't bear to think it.

"You hear that?" He angled his head.

"Sounds like the smoke alarm," one of the officers said.

His weapon at the ready, Reece used his key, unlocked and opened the door. He wouldn't be knocking and waiting for Danielle to respond when he hoped she was in the safe room. The smoke alarm blared as they eased in to clear the house. In the kitchen, smoke poured from the oven. An officer peered inside the oven, and black smoke spilled out. He turned the oven off and, using a couple of oven mitts, pulled out the lasagna.

Reece made for the hallway, clearing each room as he went. At the safe room, he peered inside. No sign that Danielle had been in the room. His heart sank even lower.

Oh Lord… Please… Show me where they are. Please keep them safe. I don't know what I'll do if something happens to them.

In the master bedroom, he found what he'd feared—signs of a struggle. The widescreen television lay in pieces on the floor. An ache stabbed through him. He could imagine Danielle using the television as a last defense—the worst kind of defense. But then…where were they?

A few minutes later, he and the police officers had cleared the house. No one was inside besides the other unconscious deputy.

"Please secure the crime scene," he said and rushed outside. He wasn't their superior, but they were first onto the scene and that was their job, anyway.

Reece rushed around the house looking for signs of the intruder or Danielle and Lucy. Of their escape or… their abduction.

The creek behind the house drew his attention.

He doubted he would find anyone there, but on the other hand, Danielle was resourceful, and if she had been able to escape the house because for some reason she couldn't make it into the safe room, then she might run into those words. Reece jogged across the backyard and into the shadowed tree canopy around the creek. He waited a moment while his eyes adjusted and, on a small bush, he spotted one lone curly blond strand.

Lucy.

His senses on alert, he continued on in the shadows of the forest. He could come across their pursuer in these woods, too. He hoped he would find the man so he could apprehend him once and for all. But he'd prefer to find Danielle and Lucy safe and sound after escaping the house. He hurried along the creek, unsure which direction they might have gone, but tried to think like Danielle.

Which way would I go if I were Danielle? That tactic didn't help, but next to the creek, he spotted footprints. Danielle. He was on the right track.

Reece continued along the creek, moving as fast as he could over the small boulders, but not too fast in case they were hiding in the underbrush or, worse, hurt. He wouldn't want to miss them.

If he'd found the signs they'd left behind, then chances were the man after them was also on their trail.

"Danielle! Lucy!" Might as well call out for them and potentially draw the pursuer's attention back to Reece, or scare the guy off. Though he wanted the man in handcuffs, he longed for Danielle and Lucy to emerge from the shadows.

Following the creek, he glanced behind the trees and rocks and underbrush. "Danielle…"

A sound drew his attention, kicking his pulse up as he held his weapon.

Lucy emerged. "Reece?" She sniffled. "Mommy's hurt."

Reece snatched Lucy up and to him, his heart lurching at her words. "Where, honey? Where is your mommy?"

Lucy pointed through the trees on the far side of the creek. That Lucy had chosen to remain in the shadows rather than go after her mother told him that danger still remained. He started to put her down.

"No, no, no. Take me to my mommy."

"Okay, honey, but I want you to be safe."

Lucy clung to him, and he knew he would never be able to let her go. He pushed through the trees, wary of the danger, and gripping his gun along with Lucy. Through the trees he spotted Danielle in the grass. Unmoving.

Oh God… Please, no…

"I'm scared," Lucy said. "Mommy told me to wait in the woods for you. That you would come for me."

Reece rushed to Danielle and dropped to his knees.

He kept Lucy's face over his shoulder, so she couldn't see her mother in case... In case...

He touched her carotid.

Still alive.

Still breathing. And now Reece, too, could breathe.

He released Lucy and turned Danielle over so he could see her face. "Danielle," he said. *Oh, Danielle.* His heart palpitated—beat erratically, pumping oddly. Adrenaline seized him. He lifted her in his arms. Ran his fingers over her soft face.

Her lashes fluttered.

"Mommy," Lucy whispered.

Of course Danielle's eyes would pop open at the sound of her daughter. Her fear-filled eyes took him in first then flicked to Lucy. Suddenly Danielle sat up and drew Lucy into her arms.

"Oh, my sweet girl. You did good. I told you Reece would find you, and you waited for him like I told you."

Reece wanted to know what happened, but it might be best to talk about it out of Lucy's hearing.

"Let's get you to the hospital. An ambulance could still be at the house."

"I'm okay. I don't need a doctor."

"For my peace of mind, Danielle."

Hugging her daughter to her, her gaze found his and the fear slowly subsided. "Okay. For your peace of mind."

Reece took her in. Was she injured? A bump on the head? He glanced at her throat. Had the intruder choked her? He realized she continued to stare at him and he allowed himself to get lost in those blue eyes. Instead of fear, compassion, along with an emotion he couldn't read, filled them.

"Thank you for coming for us. Coming when you did."

Reece silenced the voices in his head that reminded him he hadn't saved them. He hadn't gotten here in time. The man had probably been scared away when the sirens sounded. He'd run away and would only try again later. Danielle was probably thinking the same thing.

I trust you to keep us safe. Maybe I shouldn't.

Her words definitely cut through him now.

He pulled her to him, and Lucy climbed from her to him and held on. Reece held Danielle and she seemed to respond. He couldn't help himself and ran his fingers through her hair. Breathed in the scent of vanilla mixed with loam and grass.

Lucy shifted to look at him. "You shouted Mommy's name, and the man ran away. You're a good man, like Mommy said."

The words were a balm to his heart.

Next time, he might not be so fortunate.

And unfortunately, there *would* be a next time.

ELEVEN

Danielle struggled to shake off the images rushing at her. They could knock the breath from her. Her legs shook, so she leaned into Reece's sturdy form as he walked them back to the safe house. From here, she could only see the wooded area that edged the creek. Wow. She hadn't made it very far in her effort to save Lucy from the intruder. What if Reece hadn't found them? She shuddered to think of what could have happened. And this wasn't over yet.

She hoped that Reece wouldn't notice how much she relied on him to put one foot in front of another, because right now, she could barely walk. And she didn't want to show Lucy how weak she was.

As they headed toward the trees, fear inched up again. Was their stalker in those woods? Wary, she slowed.

"Hey," Reece said. "It's okay. He's gone."

"You don't know that." Danielle regretted her words. She didn't want to scare Lucy.

"I'll protect you." His frown deepened, and concern poured from his eyes.

Danielle nodded and leaned into him again as they

walked. His broad shoulders and strong arms reassured
her, and she soaked up the strength of his presence.
She couldn't help but notice her daughter did the same.
Not just now, in this instance. Lucy seemed stronger—
more healthy, more color in her cheeks, all of it—when
Reece was near. Was it some sick trick her subconscious
played on her regarding Reece's positive influence on
Lucy's young life?

Or was it some sort of weird genetic thing that caused
Lucy to thrive in his presence? Danielle didn't have
the time to ponder those secret connections. As life-
changing as they were, she had far more pressing matters. Life-and-death events continued to race at them.
She couldn't be sure what was going to happen from
one moment to the next.

But she was sure she couldn't live like this.

Nor could she stay in the safe house any longer.
Reece had to know that, too. And if they couldn't stay
there, then *where* could they stay? Where could they
go to be safe? Fear kindled again in her chest. She was
scared to death for Lucy.

"How did he find out where we are?" Danielle asked.
"That's what I want to know, Reece."

They approached the small creek where they would
have to enter the woods and cross over to the other side
to reach the house.

Reece shifted Lucy in his arms. She was like a little
monkey clinging to him. "I don't know yet. I'll have
to investigate and be more careful next time. At the
next place."

She thought he'd already been careful. "Whose house
is this, anyway? Does your department keep random

houses available for people like me who are on the run from men with guns?"

"Not my agency, but some agencies do. The place is used by my brother Ben, who is with the US Marshals. But keep that between the two of us, okay?"

"I will, but someone out there already knows. They found us, didn't they?"

"Maybe they know where you were staying, but not necessarily that it's connected to Ben's work. Still, I'll inform him of what's happened here. He might want to take this house off the list."

Lucy wanted down, so Reece released her. She reached for Danielle's hand and looked up at her, squeezing her hand as if to reassure her. The sweet gesture warmed her through and through. She couldn't let Lucy down.

God, how do I keep her safe?

Holding Lucy's hand, Danielle crossed over the small creek with her daughter. Reece crossed next to them. Close. Sturdy. Protective. How could they possibly keep going like this? With Reece by their side. After what happened today, she doubted he would leave them again. But he had a job to do. Watching over them wasn't part of that, she didn't think. She was afraid to even ask, because deep down she wanted him right here with them to keep Lucy safe until this was over.

"Tell me what happened." Reece glanced down at Lucy, then back to Danielle. She understood the question in his eyes. Did she want to talk about it in front of Lucy? Maybe she didn't, but Lucy had already lived through it, so better to get it over with now and move on.

Danielle explained about the intruder and that she'd gotten them safely out of the house. "I thought about knocking on the neighbors' doors, but this time of day, most people are at work. He could easily catch me at the door, so I opted to head to the creek and hide. Unfortunately he followed us and caught up. I knew he was close, so I made Lucy hide from him and I led him away from her."

Danielle nearly choked as she tried to form the next words.

Reece pressed his hand over her shoulder and squeezed. "It's okay, Danielle, if it's too hard to talk about."

"I need to tell you. You need to know." Danielle stopped walking and faced Reece. "He caught up to me. I ran and led him away from the creek. He toppled me. Overpowered me. He'd been trying to choke me. He kept asking me where it is and choking me. Like I could even answer him when he was cutting off my oxygen. I poked him in the eyes and escaped and ran away. He shoved me. I don't remember anything that happened after that, except…well…hearing Lucy's voice. I opened my eyes and saw the both of you."

Danielle started walking again, suddenly feeling exposed out in the open. Maybe she'd hit her head. She had no headache, but maybe that would come later.

"I'm so sorry." Reece wrapped his arm over and around her shoulder and tugged her closer as they walked. "This is all on me. I just… I'm sorry."

Danielle was sorry that it had happened, too. This whole scenario was a complete nightmare.

What had her brother gotten them into? She couldn't douse the anger that kindled against John until she reminded herself that he was in a coma and couldn't defend himself. She hoped that once he woke up, he had a good explanation.

Help me forgive him, Lord. I don't even know exactly what he's done. I only see the consequences of his actions.

They crossed over yards until they got to the backyard of the safe house. A couple of police cruisers sat in the cul-de-sac. "I don't see an ambulance."

"One arrived right after me. It must have taken one or both deputies to the hospital." He grabbed her hand as they walked.

She could feel the tension in his muscles, his entire body. He was wary and watching.

"I hope they're okay," she said. Maybe she could take them lasagna—after she cooked a whole new batch, of course—in the hospital. Still she hoped they would not have to be hospitalized and would quickly recover. Her gut clenched. They had been hurt because of her and Lucy's need for protection.

"Did you recognize the man after you?" Reece's question broke through her anguished thoughts.

"No. It wasn't the man from the campsite."

Reece paused next to her and kept her from walking forward. He turned her shoulders so she faced him. "I won't leave you again, Danielle. I promise."

"But what about your job, Reece? You can't investigate or help solve this if you're only...if you're our protector." Reece could end up hurt like the deputies, but on the other side of that, Danielle needed someone to help her protect Lucy.

His jaw worked back and forth, the familiar action causing memories to flood her.

"I don't want you to be obligated to protect us." Oh, now. Why had she said that?

Hurt surged in his gaze. "Obligated. Is that why you think I'm here with you?"

"I mean… Isn't it?"

Reece searched her gaze, appearing to work past the hurt and contemplate his reply. Or maybe search his heart to find the truth. "No. Realistically, another agent or office might handle things differently. Or a different agency might assign someone to you. I've kept my supervisor informed, but Danielle… I'm here with you because it's…well…*you*."

"You're saying that if I were someone else, you wouldn't be here? I don't buy that. You would protect whoever you needed to protect, Reece."

What are you doing, Danielle? Reece is the best chance you have to protect Lucy. But she wanted— needed—to know the depth of his commitment. After what happened today, she might need to find a different way for her and Lucy, though she had no idea what that way would be. Who would be more protective than her brother, John, who was in a coma right now?

Aware that Lucy stared up at the two of them, her big blue eyes registering each and every word, Danielle realized she shouldn't have this conversation with Reece at the moment. She hadn't meant to. The words just burst out. She regretted asking him, forcing him to respond. She wasn't sure she could trust anything he said right now. She started forward with Lucy.

Reece caught her wrist and held her back. "I would do my job, Danielle. Yes. But *you* know why I'm here with you, and it doesn't have a thing to do with obligation."

Somewhere near the house, someone shouted. She couldn't understand the words, but Lucy drew her attention. She reached up to Reece, and he lifted her in his arms.

Oh...no... Reece couldn't have figured out that Lucy was his daughter. If only he knew... No, it couldn't be that. Reece cared about Danielle; he cared about them both. Deeply. She saw that in his eyes and knew that to her bones. But she couldn't allow that care to grow into something more. After this was over...it was over.

Still, Reece needed to know whom he was protecting.

Now would be the moment for Danielle to tell him, except Lucy was here.

"Mommy? I took a picture of the man with your phone."

Danielle gasped. "Oh, good, sweetie, let me see."

A picture could go a long way to identify him. Danielle found the last image on her cell and showed it to Reece. "Well?"

Reece stared at the image and slowly nodded. "That's the man I encountered at John's house."

An explosion rocked the ground. Reece covered her and Lucy with his body.

Protecting Danielle. Protecting his daughter.

Reece didn't want to hurt these two precious people as he covered them with his body. He wanted to protect them. He willed himself to protect them as the explosion rocked their world.

He waited until his heart rate slowed, his breathing slowed, then slowly, painfully lifted his head and peered at the chaos surrounding them.

Flames engulfed the safe house. His gut clenched and twisted.

How much more do we have to take, Lord?

Reece shifted away from Danielle and Lucy to allow them freedom to move. "Are…are you all right?" His voice was unsteady.

She shook her head and stared at him as if in shock.

In Danielle's eyes, he could see the desperate worry she had for her child. Lucy might not be able to hold up to so much drama. Much had happened in a short time—and even he struggled to wrap his mind around it. How much more could a little girl, one who had a heart condition, take?

Time to move. Sirens rang out in the distance. More emergency vehicles were on the way.

Reece leaned in to speak. "I would prefer to stay here in the grass—get our bearings, let you get steady legs—but someone could be watching. We need to move."

Danielle's eyes widened with fear, and she nodded her agreement. She scrambled to her feet along with Reece. He scooped Lucy up and reached out his hand. Danielle took it without hesitation. He led her around neighboring backyards. He hoped for not only firetrucks but ambulances. Right before the explosion, he thought he'd heard someone shout…

"Bomb!"

Now he realized that had been the word. He hoped that law enforcement and anyone else who was there to investigate what had happened had made it out of the house and away from the explosion before it was too late. As he approached the cul-de-sac, he spotted his NPS vehicle—obliterated by a chunk of the house's roof sinking into the hood.

Great. His company car was toast. But in the scheme of things, that didn't matter. The vehicle could be replaced. Lives could not. At least Lucy and Danielle were safe. He worried about anyone who might have been in the house.

But the sight of his vehicle punched him in the gut, and he hesitated, unsure what his next steps should be. He wasn't able to put Danielle and Lucy into the vehicle and go somewhere safe. For the first time in a long time, he had no idea what he was going to do next, and he prided himself on always thinking ahead.

Lord, guide me. Direct my path. Help me keep them safe.

"What now?" Danielle asked.

He hated hearing the utter defeat in her tone and knew she referred to the fact that their transportation was gone.

Along with Danielle's tablet. Their luggage. At least John's laptop had already been handed over to Reece's tech guy.

Time for Reece to reach deep down and man up. Be the man that Danielle needed. The protector she and Lucy needed. He inhaled and lifted his shoulders. "If I can get us a ride back to my house, I can get my personal vehicle. And as for the picture that Lucy took, I'll send this image to the right people to search for this man. Finding out who he is will help us to nail him and be done with this for good."

Danielle nodded, but her furrowed brows told him nothing he said had eased her concern.

"But still, Reece. Even if we go get your vehicle, then what? Where can we go that's safe? We don't know how he found us here. And I say 'he' as in the *one* guy, but

I'm not sure that both men did not find me here. I don't have a clue if they're on the same or different teams. One abducted us but shot John, and the other guy prefers to shoot at us, choke me and blow up houses."

Different tactics. Reece hung his head, and when he lifted it again, he watched the fire truck rumble by them to the house. Emergency workers and police officers had congregated in the cul-de-sac and waited on the firemen. Reece sighed, feeling the defeat reach inside and grip his bones.

"I wish your brother would wake up and explain all this." How could John have dragged his amazing sister and precious young niece into this? Reece shook his head as he watched the water finally flowing onto the house but late, much too late. Exhaustion weighing on him, he shook his head.

The world around him shifted into a tunnel, everything outside the small circle that included Danielle and Lucy seeming fuzzy and distant.

Get a grip. Danielle's pursuers—either of them—could be nearby and watching.

Reece had to find a new safe place and fast. He couldn't take her to any of his family—his brother Ryan and his new wife, Tori, were expecting a baby. His sister, Katelyn, was busy planning her upcoming wedding, and he didn't want to distract or endanger her. Ben was off protecting a witness. Reece wouldn't put his parents in danger. The family lake house on Mount Shasta Lake was out of the question, too, because they could be found there as had already been proven.

"Come on." He tugged Danielle forward. Lucy remained snuggled against him. If by holding her, he could offer her the strength and protection that she needed to remain calm and healthy and strong, he would hold her forever…only he couldn't actually hold her forever. She didn't belong to him.

He doubted he would ever be so fortunate to have a daughter as precious as this little girl.

"Where are we going?" Danielle asked.

He didn't answer because he didn't know yet. He was making this up as he went. He wove in front of a slowly approaching vehicle. And waved just in case the driver was focused on the house instead of people. The vehicle stopped.

The man's eyes were wide, his expression grim, as he opened the door and stepped out.

His brother Ben's eyes were filled with the glow of the house fire, then his gaze drifted over to Reece, Danielle and Lucy.

"What are you doing here?" Reece's voice cracked with emotion. "I thought you…" *were on protection duty*.

"My schedule got switched up." Ben looked at the house then back to Reece. "It looks like it was a good thing." An emotion Reece couldn't read filled Ben's gaze and somehow made Reece feel uncomfortable and awkward.

Oh, he got it. Reece looked like a man with a pretend family.

Still, he wouldn't release Lucy. Not as long as she needed him.

TWELVE

Danielle sat in the back seat of the big white Suburban. Reece's brother Ben had called in an order at an Italian restaurant, and they had eaten quickly at a picnic table at a park along the way toward their secret destination. Now Lucy napped with the seat leaned back while Danielle listened to the voice mail left by a nurse from Lucy's doctor's office. The nurse was returning Danielle's call. Of course, they would have to play phone tag. But the message didn't relay any concern for Lucy's health, and that reassured Danielle.

Reece had explained to her where they were heading, but she was too exhausted, too traumatized, frankly, to comprehend his explanation. She was left with nothing except to completely trust him, and he had already built that trust when it came to their lives. He couldn't have known that the safe house, with two deputies guarding them, would not be enough. None of them could have known. Danielle's trust in him didn't waver because of it. In fact, she trusted him even more because now he knew more, as did she. That whoever was after them would go to great lengths to get to them.

Danielle had given her statement to officers at the

scene, and then Reece and Ben had whisked her and Lucy away. Night had fallen, and a big full moon rose in the sky.

If these two men—Special Agent Reece Bradley and Ben, a U.S. Marshal who was accustomed to protecting people—couldn't keep Danielle and Lucy safe, then she didn't know who could.

God, I know You sent them. You had to have sent them.

The reasons why God would need to send such men terrified her. Still, at the moment she couldn't be in safer hands. If she was going to get some rest, this was the time.

Danielle leaned the seat back and allowed herself to sleep. She would need her strength over the next few days—*God, please let this just be over, and sooner rather than later*—in order to take care of Lucy and be the mother she needed to be to see her precious little girl happy and safe. Who would think that would be so hard?

In fact, it had been hard before this trip to see John had turned their lives into a dangerous game of cloak-and-dagger.

She'd continued to call and check in at the hospital and learned there was no change in John's health. She wished they could be there in the room with him, but it wasn't possible now. In order to relax and sleep, Danielle forced her mind to happier times. To swinging with Lucy at the park. She didn't go so far back with her thoughts that Tom was in them, because somehow, she almost felt like she was betraying her late husband given the feelings she battled every moment in Reece's presence.

* * *

Danielle woke up to the shift in movement. Ben's Suburban had slowed. Reece reached forward in his seat to charge his cell. Had he slept at all? Neither he nor Ben spoke—probably wanting to remain quiet while she and Lucy slept.

The headlights revealed a dense forest lining the road. Then suddenly, Ben turned off the headlights.

"What are you doing?" she asked. Then she noticed Ben had donned night-vision goggles.

The only light was from the night sky. Both men peered out the window to the left as Ben turned down another road—almost invisible due to the trees. He stopped and got out. She heard clinking, and then he opened a gate. She strained to see even that. He got back in and steered them forward, then closed the gate behind them. As Ben drove, the SUV dipped down with the road. The moon had long drifted out of her line of sight, and now she could see the stars shining in the darkest part of the night.

What was that saying again? The darkest part of the night was when the lights shined the brightest. They trailed the road for a mile or so, then Ben parked. Reece shifted to look in the back seat. The vehicle remained too dark, but she could feel his eyes on her.

"I can't see," she whispered. "Where are we going? What are we doing?"

"We're here." Reece spoke quietly.

Ben turned on the dashboard lights, and Danielle glanced at her daughter.

Lucy hadn't woken up yet. Good. Danielle pressed a finger to her lips and looked at Reece. He motioned for her to remain in the vehicle. He and Ben pulled out guns, opened doors and stepped out then quietly closed the doors behind them. They moved toward…toward what? A tree? Then swept the perimeter.

Next they climbed steps up the tree. What? Danielle followed their forms up toward…a tree house?

A tree house.

Danielle couldn't have been more surprised. She guessed using Fort Knox as a safe house just wasn't an option.

Within a few minutes, the lights in the tree house came on. Reece bounded down the staircase and hiked back to the vehicle, then opened Danielle's door. She twisted to climb out, and when she dropped to the ground, her legs almost collapsed beneath her. Reece caught her up against him and held her there. Danielle had no business getting this comfortable with him. Against him. In his arms.

But… Oh… She pressed her forehead into his shoulder and soaked in everything about him. His strength. Protection. Reassurance. Security… How she needed all of it in this moment.

Danielle lifted her face, expecting Reece to step away.

After all, it was time to get Lucy into bed, safe and sound at least for one night. But Reece didn't move. Instead, he looked down into her face and peered into her eyes. His eyes were bright even in the shadows. Behind him, the starry sky stared down at her as if joining Reece in perusing Danielle's open soul.

"Danielle," he whispered. "I hope you know I'll do anything to keep you and Lucy safe. *Anything.*"

She was starting to understand that about Reece. "Yes, I know. I trust you with our lives. But I can't lie… I'm still scared of what comes next. I'm scared for you—I don't want you to get hurt while protecting us. And I'm scared for Lucy."

She averted her gaze, but he gently lifted her chin, forcing her eyes back to him. Danielle looked into his eyes, his face in the shadows. She didn't need light to know his jaw was chiseled and his features handsome.

"I failed you today." Pain filled his words. "But I won't let that happen again."

And then determination replaced that pain.

"Why, Reece? Why do you care so much?" She regretted the question. Did it matter that she knew? Yes, yes it did… And again, that nudge to tell him the truth gnawed at her heart. What kind of person was she to keep this truth from him?

Terrified. Protective.

He lowered his chin and angled toward her, inching closer.

She couldn't resist the draw of him, the memories that flooded her, the knowledge of who this man was. He hadn't meant to hurt her. She knew that. And at this moment, she couldn't resist this connection, the pull he had over her.

She met him the rest of the way, pressing her lips into his, feeling the tenderness there, the care and emotion. Her mind screamed at her while her heart clung to something desperately wanted. Desperately needed. Though deep inside she knew this shouldn't happen between them…it was happening nonetheless.

The kiss, that was.

The emotional connection.

And there it was. Danielle had set herself up to be hurt once again, though she'd determined not to.

"Mommy?" The sweet, soft voice gasped with excitement. "You're kissing Reece. Is he going to be my new daddy?"

Oh no… Danielle had set Lucy up to get hurt.

Lucy had wanted Reece to carry her into the house, despite Danielle's protest. He marched up to the porch holding this little girl to whom he'd grown inexplicably attached. Ben stood at the top of the steps and watched Reece as he carried Lucy.

Lucy's words had clung to him. *Mommy? You're kissing Reece. Is he going to be my new daddy?*

The child's words—filled with hope—had wrapped around his heart and filled him with joy and warmth and pain all at once. And that left him confused and tormented.

Danielle hadn't answered her daughter but instead had simply redirected her with something about staying in a tree house—what a novelty that was.

Within the massive branches of a sturdy oak tree, the tree house was hidden well. Ben had found this place—secluded and protected in a gated community of tree house dwellers.

Reece's only concern was that Lucy might possibly fall, but the tree house was built with safety and prevention in mind.

Ben led Reece to a small bedroom with two twin beds. "Lucy and Danielle can stay here."

To Danielle, he said, "I'm sorry there isn't more room."

"Don't apologize." Danielle stood in the middle of the room and took it all in. "This is perfect. I want to be with Lucy to protect her. I don't need a separate room."

Reece laid Lucy on the bed, and Danielle pulled the quilt in rustic earth tones over her to make her comfortable. She eased onto the edge of the twin bed and gently brushed a few wisps of Lucy's curly hair from her forehead. He waited to see if Lucy would look at him, but she didn't. She hadn't spoken a word to him since the awkward moment between Danielle and Reece when they had shared a kiss. Awkward for them, something entirely different for her.

And for that he could kick himself.

Why, oh why had he created the opportunity for them to share a kiss?

Maybe because he cared much too deeply for Danielle and had been a fool. He couldn't stop himself. But he was being selfish to kiss her, and he knew it.

He wanted to punch something. Danielle was vulnerable, and he'd taken advantage of that. On the other hand, he'd wanted her to know the depth of his commitment to keeping them safe. He hadn't been thinking, at least not with his head, but instead with his heart, and his reassurances to her had come out of him with a kiss.

Why did his attempt to reassure her, to comfort her, end in hurting her? He hadn't intended that.

He lingered at the door, then Danielle glanced up at him, exhaustion and frustration in her eyes. Maybe lingering regret for the kiss, too. He took her cue and closed the door.

Arms crossed, Ben stared at him from across the room in the kitchen. Reece let his gaze take in the small tree house—most of the space was taken up by the kitchen, dining and living area. A porch around half of it, and two small bedrooms. A bathroom near the bedroom where Danielle and Lucy stayed. Windows everywhere. He understood the reasons for the windows. Why live in a tree house if you couldn't take in the view? When he'd finished assessing all possible entries and exits, he realized that Ben hadn't budged. His brother continued watching him. Obviously he had something on his mind, and Reece had the strong feeling it had nothing to do with his self-imposed protection duty.

But he didn't want to talk where Danielle or Lucy could hear. Ben showed Reece a bedroom where they could sleep. Ben followed him in and then closed the door behind him.

He leaned against it as if he had no intention of letting Reece leave without a conversation. "Tomorrow, I have a friend who will bring a German shepherd."

"I don't know if Danielle will like that. She might be afraid for Lucy's sake."

"There's no better home security."

"Wait, this place has a security alarm, doesn't it?"

"At the gate."

Reece frowned. "Why did you bring us here?"

"You know as well as I do that anyone with know-how can break through a security alarm, which means you shouldn't trust them or count on them. There are motion detectors—the lights will come on. And a trained dog will bark and protect."

"Trained dogs will protect their family. We aren't the dog's family."

Ben chuckled. "So you *are* a family now?"

"What? No… Danielle… I told you how this all came about. Now, about the dog, I don't think it's a good idea."

"My friend will stay with the dog. She'll be part of your security detail."

"In this small space?"

"Let's hope this doesn't take that long. In the meantime, I have to leave as soon as she gets here. I have a witness to protect."

Reece hung his head, gathering the words, then lifted his face again. "Thanks, Ben. I don't know what I would have done if you hadn't shown up when you did. I was… I was out of options. Out of hope. I couldn't let them down."

"You told me some of what's going on with Danielle, but I think you're keeping a *big* part of it from me." The look Ben gave him could only be read one way.

"There's nothing between me and Danielle. There can't be." Yeah, and he'd kissed her. What a hypocrite.

"There's *someone* between you, Reece. Or… Wait…" Ben's gaze shifted as if incredulous. "You don't know."

THIRTEEN

Danielle tossed and turned in the small, squeaky twin bed. Good thing she'd slept on the drive, but that had only been a few hours of sleep. Restless sleep at that.

And then he'd kissed her.

Or rather, she'd kissed him. He'd only invited her to a kiss, but he hadn't left her any options. No options at all when he was so close and she'd wanted that kiss. He was simply responding to the need in her. She'd needed more than physical protection, she'd needed the emotional connection…so he'd touched her lips and her heart.

And Lucy had seen that kiss and had expectations now.

Danielle could not hurt her daughter again. Falling for Reece, going down that road, could lead to more tragedy. She and Lucy had already been through too much and were still going through too much.

She stared at the ceiling of logs and turned her heart to God.

Lord, how did we get here? How did I get to this place? Sleeping in a tree house. Lucy's father out there, though he didn't know.

His brother Ben hanging around for who knew how long. And no answers to this dangerous mystery in sight.

And Lucy. Poor, sweet Lucy. She didn't deserve this. Danielle's concern for her daughter increased with every new twist in their unfortunate story.

Lucy had curled into her usual fetal position and didn't move the rest of the night. Danielle should know, since she'd been awake and was surprised she hadn't woken Lucy with all her own tossing and turning.

A dog's bark startled Danielle. Morning light poured into the room. Panic swelled in her chest. Heart pounding, she scrambled out of bed and peered out the window, momentarily disoriented until she remembered the tree house.

Below her a dog and woman bounded up the steps.

What in the world? Fear swept over her. Who was this new intruder? A neighbor coming to check on them? How could they keep safe unless no one knew they were here?

"Mommy? Where are we?"

Danielle turned to see Lucy sitting up in bed, her blond curls falling over her face. "It's okay, honey. Don't you remember? Last night we came to sleep in a tree house. See the leaves on the tree? We're *in* the tree. Isn't that cool?"

Lucy rubbed her eyes then stared out the window as if trying to get her bearings.

Smiling, Danielle remained next to the window and tried to project a calm, even manner. She did Lucy no favors by constantly panicking and functioning in a barely controllable state of fear. So she would get her calm on, inside and out.

There's nothing to worry about. Ben and Reece are here.

This time, the dog's bark came from inside the house. Danielle almost jumped at the sound. Men's voices mingled with a woman's voice. But they weren't shouting, nothing angry sounding, so that was good, wasn't it?

Danielle wished that she and Lucy had clothes to change into. They'd grabbed food, but had all been too shell-shocked and too exhausted to think about a change of clothes and… Well, maybe this place at least had toiletries.

She finger-combed her hair. "Come on, honey. Let's go to the bathroom. Maybe we can round up toothbrushes. Wash our face and comb our hair."

"Okay, Mommy. And I'm hungry, too. But I heard a dog. Can we see it?"

The dog barked and then growled. Danielle stiffened, and her breathing hitched. What now?

She caught Lucy when her daughter raced for the door. "Wait here. I need to make sure it's safe."

She cracked the door to peer out then saw the dog playing with the woman and Ben. Reece was more cautious but stuck his hand out for the German shepherd to sniff.

Reece's eyes shifted toward the door. He'd seen her, but said nothing. Danielle closed the door and pressed her back against it.

"Mommy, what's wrong?"

"Nothing's wrong, sweetie." What was a German shepherd doing here? She got the sense it was a trained attack dog.

An attack dog around her baby? Not happening.

A gentle knock came at the door. "Danielle, it's okay. You can come out now."

She cracked the door. "What's with the attack dog?"

Reece had crossed his arms. "Ben's idea of extra protection."

"I don't like it," she said. "The dog could hurt Lucy. Attack dogs aren't...they aren't pets."

"Don't worry. I've been assured that Eve will be staying in the small RV she brought along with her dog. He's just an extra measure of protection, and according to Ben there's no better protection than a guard dog to alert you when other systems fail."

Danielle thought her heart would stop beating. Oh no...had it come to that?

Lucy opened the door all the way and lifted her arms to Reece, who tugged her up and into his arms.

Danielle hated the tears surging in her eyes for a million reasons.

"If having the dog here bothers you that much, I can send them away."

"It's not that. Or not *just* that." She swiped at her eyes. "So embarrassing."

"You're just exhausted, as we all are."

She nodded, appreciating his understanding. She laughed hysterically. "We're so desperate that we need an attack dog to protect us."

Lucy lifted her head.

Why had she said that? She hadn't meant to scare her daughter any more than she had a right to be.

The German shepherd approached and sniffed at Reece's heels. The dog's presence made Danielle nervous, though she'd had pets as a kid.

"His name is Buck," the woman said from behind Reece.

"Like in *Call of the Wild*?" Lucy asked.

"I'm Eve, by the way," the slim brunette said.

"And I'm Lucy. This is my mom, Mommy. She read me that book a few months ago."

Danielle reached out her hand to shake Eve's. "Danielle."

Eve's smile was beautiful. She was beautiful. One of Ben's friend's? Or Reece's? The woman crouched and ran her hands over Buck's head and around his ears. He panted and relaxed.

"Buck wants to be your friend, Lucy."

Danielle stiffened. She wasn't sure she felt comfortable with this situation. Fortunately Reece glanced to Danielle for her permission.

"I'll crouch and hold on to Lucy while she pets Buck. How about that?" His tone reassured her.

"Okay."

Reece got on the floor and, as promised, he held on to her daughter. *His* daughter, though he didn't know yet.

Buck sniffed Lucy, panted and wagged his tail. Danielle relaxed as Lucy giggled. Still, the dog was big, so big compared to her little girl, and he could hurt her.

"Well, I think Buck is acclimated to this new property, and I'll just take him down now and we'll walk the perimeter. Let him mark the area that we'll be guarding."

Eve gave Buck a command, and his demeanor instantly shifted. He stiffened and his ears were up and alert. He followed her out through the small living area and exited the front door.

Only then did Danielle relax.

"Mommy, Mommy! I love Buck. Can we get a Buck when we get home?"

Reece chuckled, the deep timbre filling Danielle with a feeling she couldn't describe. But she knew she wanted—no, needed—more of that in her life.

"We can talk about it later," she said. "Now, go on into the bathroom and wash your face. I'll be right in."

Reece released Lucy, and her little pitter-pattering feet carried her into the bathroom.

Danielle waited until she had Reece's full attention. "Was this really necessary?"

"It can't hurt to have the extra protection, can it? Eve and Buck will hang out below the tree house. You and Lucy won't have to interact with them much, if at all."

Danielle nodded, still trying to come to grips with their precarious situation. "We need a few things."

"I understand. Ben is going to run out to get those things for you. I'll need your clothing sizes and a list of what you might need."

"Will that be a risk to us? He could lead someone back here."

"Ben does this for a living. He's the best at what he does. In the meantime, I'll work on breakfast."

"Don't tell me this place was stocked?"

"It wasn't, but Ben picked up enough at the local store. He's waiting for your essentials list now. Clothing, toiletries, even special groceries or other items for Lucy." Reece winked.

The birthday cake she'd made had been destroyed. She wasn't sure what had happened to the presents Reece had planned to buy. Maybe they had been crushed in his vehicle. And what if she made Lucy another cake, and it happened all over again? Honestly, it might be best to wait until they were through this to throw Lucy a party. In fact, she wouldn't bring it up or bake a cake until she was sure they could actually celebrate.

And right now…she wasn't sure about anything.

"And breakfast," Ben called. "I'm waiting on breakfast."

Danielle sighed and then made to move past Reece to assist Lucy. He caught her wrist. "After breakfast, we need to talk."

The intensity in his eyes drilled down into her soul. She feared she knew exactly what he wanted to talk about—her big lie of omission.

She nodded slowly.

While Danielle and Lucy ate bacon, eggs and toast, Reece left them inside and walked out with Ben, who'd scarfed the breakfast up in ten seconds flat after receiving a call.

"I gotta go." Ben rushed down the steps. "I have to hurry if I'm going to get your list and then get back to my own schedule."

"Thanks for this, bro." Ben had shown up right when Reece was almost at the end of his rope. After he'd taken Danielle to the hospital to see John, he'd contacted Ben about using a safe house. Ben had come to check and see if Reece had gotten settled into the house… only the house was gone by the time Ben got there. Regardless, Reece didn't know how to adequately thank him. "I owe you."

"You can make it up to me later," Ben called over his shoulder and threw in a teasing wink. They were brothers. Reece knew they would be there for each other no matter what, and no one ever owed anyone a thing for it.

Thank You, Lord. Keep Ben safe out there in his own world of protecting people.

He watched his brother stop by the small travel RV and speak to Eve, who had been recommended by a group of security specialists. This wasn't the first time she'd worked with Ben to guard someone in need of protection.

Considering that Clay and Dale, two good deputies, had been taken out of commission for their protective duties, Reece decided the guard dog for hire was actually a great idea. To that end, he hoped no one would find them here. He'd contacted the hospital to ask about the deputies, and they had both recovered and been released.

He had a call in to Anthony about the laptop and also wanted to ask about possible ways they could have been discovered at the safe house. Maybe the laptop itself had some sort of tracking that had been hacked, and that's how Danielle and Lucy had been found. Maybe the laptop is what had brought the criminals to John's house, but they had not been able to find it because it had been tucked away in Lucy's special hiding place.

In that case, their discovery at the safe house was all on him. He shouldn't have allowed her to look at it first—it hadn't rendered anything of value that had benefited them, at least worth the risk keeping the laptop had posed.

Ben climbed into his SUV parked next to a Jeep. He'd taken care of getting another vehicle delivered for Reece, since he would be leaving them. The guy had his act together. Ben got out and clomped back up the steps to the tree house.

He pressed car keys into Reece's hand. "I almost forgot to hand these over."

"You've outdone yourself, Ben. You make me feel inadequate."

"Don't worry. You'll get your chance to pay me back. When I'm in the middle of protecting a lovely lady whom I've fallen in love with, I'm sure I'll be a bit more clumsy, too."

Reece tensed. "What are you talking about?"

"Got to go." He rushed back down the steps again.

"Be prepared to answer when you get back." Reece doubted Ben would have an answer, though.

Ben had never explained about his statement last night—that there was someone between Reece and Danielle—leaving Reece with only, "You'll have to figure this out on your own, bro."

Like Reece needed that kind of cryptic statement in the middle of everything going on.

A knot grew in his throat. He thought he might know exactly to what Ben had referred. He watched his brother drive away then headed back into the house. Danielle was at the kitchen sink washing dishes. He sidled up next to her and assisted.

"You don't have to wash the dishes," he said.

"You cooked, so I'll do the dishes." She smiled up at him. "Then tonight, after I cook, you can do the dishes."

"Deal," he said.

She put away the last plate.

Turning to him, she hitched her hip against the counter and crossed her arms. "I have to say, this is an unusual place to hide. A tree house, of all places."

I have to say, I love that sparkle in your striking blue

eyes. "Yeah, well, we owe Ben for sweeping in to save the day and move us to a new safe house."

He scratched his head.

"What? You were fresh out of safe houses?"

"Fresh out? I don't keep safe houses. I don't usually…"

"I get it. You're not usually on protection duty."

"And frankly, last night with the explosion, everything that happened, I was feeling at a loss." He regretted being that transparent with her. She needed to know that he would come through for her.

"Thank you for that."

Confused, he gazed at her. "For what?"

"For being honest with me. It lets me know…well, that you're human."

He chuckled. "You weren't sure if I was human?" Even after that colossal mistake of a kiss?

A grin hitched her cheeks. "You know what I mean. I appreciate your being honest with me."

Would she press him again about why her? He wasn't sure he could put it into words, but he sensed in his bones that she understood.

They had a connection. Past, present…and he didn't know about the future.

Lucy hopped from her chair at the table and ran over to him. She thrust her arms up to him, her big blue eyes filled with wonder and hope. Warmth curled around his heart. Of course he would never deny her.

He lifted her in his arms.

"Can we go for a walk?" she asked.

He'd been afraid she might ask that, but he appreciated the interruption. He'd told Danielle they needed to talk, but he wasn't ready for that conversation. Not yet. "I'll ask Eve if she thinks it's okay, or even a bad idea. Wait here?"

Lucy nodded, and he set her down. Danielle shoved her hair behind her ears and led Lucy over to the windows. Reece bounded down the steps and crossed over to the small RV, where he knocked on the door. No one answered. He needed to have a conversation with Eve anyway, about any signals—what kind of barks he could expect that would alert them to trouble.

A sound behind him drew him around. He'd already grabbed his weapon.

"Hold it there, cowboy." Eve strolled up. She gave the command to release Buck, and he rushed forward, but his demeanor was one of a dog greeting a friend. Reece crouched and gave Buck a belly rub. "Lucy wants to know if it's okay to go for a walk. I would like to walk around the grounds. Get a tour. I have a feeling Danielle wants that, too, just so she can feel comfortable."

"We just returned from our hourly perimeter check, and all appears well. But you're the one who has to make that call on whether to take those you protect on a walk out in the woods. You're the one who knows what you're dealing with. How determined are the people who want to find this woman? Or are they after her child?"

"Her child? No. I can't tell you much other than they're determined."

"You said 'they'—just how many are there?"

"There could be two different men. Their tactics are different."

"You're not telling me more because it's on a need-to-know basis, or you don't know yourself?"

"I don't know if they are working together or separately. My guess is two different purposes. And yes, it's a guess at this moment." His shoulder shifted down. He hated how much he didn't know about this situation. The truth of her last words grated across his nerves.

"Anything else you can tell me?"

Reece angled his head up at the tree house. He couldn't see Danielle or Lucy watching him through the window, but he sensed they were. "Yes. The last two places got blown up."

The way Eve's eyes narrowed told him that Ben had not shared that with her. His brother had left Reece to share what he would.

Eve remained silent for a few moments, then finally said, "Well, Buck isn't an explosives dog. But he'll warn you, and he'll attack." Her gaze lifted to the tree house.

Reece followed her gaze. Danielle and Lucy had moved out of the house and now stood on the porch looking down at them.

"If it makes you feel better, these woods are thick. The advantage is that no one can get close enough to see them. The disadvantage is there are places to hide in case someone knows exactly where the woman and child are."

Nodding, he took in her words. "For now, I think it's okay to walk the area and get a feel for what's out there." In case of the worst-case scenario—if Danielle found herself needing to escape with Lucy again.

And after that walk, then he would talk to her. Tell her everything that happened before. And if he did, then maybe she would open up to him and tell him the truth.

FOURTEEN

By the time they'd walked the grounds, which amounted to about ten densely wooded acres, Danielle was winded. Lucy had walked much of it herself. It was good for her to get out and enjoy the beautiful day and the gorgeous woods filled with pines and a few hardwoods here and there. Lots of needles carpeted the ground, but in places thick underbrush grew, so they tried to skirt around those. A creek cut across the property, too. Boulders here and there. Lucy was getting fresh air and exercise, and for a few minutes at least, she and Danielle could forget why they were here.

Eventually Lucy ended up in Danielle's arms, and then, of course, Reece's, too. They took turns holding Lucy. She didn't weigh much and was easy enough to carry except when traipsing across uneven terrain. Lucy rode piggyback at times and giggled a lot.

Danielle loved that sound—this was just perfect.

Thank You, Lord.

They'd needed this place and this day.

And they'd needed Reece. He made Danielle feel safe, and with the added protection Buck and his handler, Eve, provided, Danielle could almost breathe a sigh of relief. But they couldn't live this way. This had to end soon. Somehow.

Some way.

They finally found their way back to the tree house. Danielle followed Reece up the steps and smiled at Lucy, who peered at Danielle over her shoulder.

That image of her smiling, happy daughter in Reece's arms would forever be burned in her mind and heart. If only she could cherish it and not feel one ounce of pain to go with it.

The sound of a vehicle approaching drew their attention. The trees and terrain obscured much of the mile drive to the tree house, so they couldn't see the vehicle.

"Who's coming?" Lucy asked.

"I don't know yet." Danielle watched the drive as she continued up the steps.

"Let's get inside." Reece urged Lucy through the door.

He'd kept his tone even for Lucy's sake, but Danielle sensed his concern. She entered the house then turned to peer outside.

A white SUV emerged from the trees along the curvy drive.

"Ben." Breath whooshed from Reece. "I'd almost forgotten he would be coming back here."

Relief coursed through Danielle, too. "He must be back with our list."

"Does that mean I get new clothes, Mommy?"

Danielle allowed Lucy back onto the deck, where she jumped up and down, excited at the prospect of something new to wear. "I hope Uncle Ben got me pink, Mommy."

Uncle Ben...

How had Lucy taken to calling Reece's brother uncle?
Oh Lord, what am I going to do?

Reece bounded down the steps to assist Ben in carrying up the sacks.

Lots and lots of white paper sacks.

Just how long did Reece think they would be here? It wasn't like Danielle and Lucy were in some witness protection program where their names would be changed and they would start a whole new life and therefore need a whole new identity and whole new wardrobe with it. A sinking feeling grew in her gut, but she forced a smile as Reece and Ben carried the sacks up.

She was grateful. What would she do? Where would she be if not for Reece showing up at that gas station and then deciding to follow her? She held the door for the men as they entered the house. Reece set sacks on the dining table.

"Where do you want these?" Ben lifted sacks.

"In the room we're using." She wouldn't call it their bedroom as if claiming any kind of ownership. She didn't want to speak words that suggested a long-term stay. Reece and Ben left again. Another round of bags? Lucy dashed to the bedroom, no doubt to open bags and look for pink clothes.

Danielle unpacked the groceries that Ben had bought for them. Danielle heard Lucy squeal. "Uncle Ben" had done well.

Ben entered the house and set more bags on the floor. He pressed his hands against a chair back and watched her as if waiting for her attention. She paused from putting groceries away and acknowledged him. "Thank you for this. For everything."

He smiled. "You're more than welcome. I hope to

see you and Lucy on the other side of this. I have other business that needs my attention, so I'll say my good-byes now."

Danielle clasped her hands in front of her. For some reason, she felt like she should say more. "I don't know what Lucy and I would have done in this situation without your and Reece's help."

"I'd say it's all part of the job, but it's more than that." Ben winked at her and turned his back to walk out, leaving her to ponder his comment. Reece followed him out.

Danielle finished putting the groceries away and found Lucy eyeing a pretty outfit she'd laid out on the bed. "Mommy? I want to take a bath before I get dressed. Would that be okay? I don't want to get the clothes dirty."

"I think that's a great idea."

Danielle spent the rest of the day pretending all was well as she braided Lucy's hair. Ben had bought some pink ribbons, too, as Reece had suggested. And a new set of dangly earrings for Danielle. How strange it felt to be spoiled under these circumstances. So thoughtful of them.

When she and Lucy emerged from the bedroom, clean and in their newly purchased clothes, Reece was putting the finishing touches on the meal he'd prepared—spaghetti with meatballs and a salad.

This felt nothing at all like a safe house and far too much like…like they were a family.

Oh, Reece… If only.

"Will Eve be joining us?"

"I invited her, but no. She said she has a routine she likes to keep with Buck while they're working."

Oh. Well, that smashed her imaginings of a normal world without danger waiting in the shadows to grab them.

Reece set the bowl of salad on the table next to the bigger bowl of pasta. "Plus, she doesn't like to let her guard down—after all, that's why she's here."

Isn't that why you're here, too?

After dinner, Lucy yawned, and Danielle put her to bed and kissed her good-night. "Aren't you going to bed, Mommy?"

"Not yet, Pumpkin. I need to talk to Reece." She left the door cracked so she could hear if Lucy needed her, but she didn't want Lucy to hear their conversation.

Reece was cleaning up the dishes. "Hey, wait a minute. I thought I was supposed to do that. In fact, I was supposed to cook dinner, too, but you beat me to it."

He shrugged. "It's my pleasure to cook and to clean up. You needed to spend time with Lucy."

Danielle helped him with the last few dishes. "Thanks for dinner. You're a great cook."

"Thanks." He laughed. "You're the only person who would ever say that."

Tell him. You need to tell him the truth.

"Earlier I told you that we need to talk." Reece folded the dish towel and set it on the counter. "Now's the time."

I was afraid you'd say that. She was so torn about what to do—tell him the truth or protect herself and Lucy from the pain that would follow.

Lord, why does everything have to be so hard?

Reece moved to the front door and opened it, gesturing for her to step out onto the porch. "It's a nice night. Let's talk out here."

"Is it safe out here?"

"I thought you'd prefer talking away from Lucy so she doesn't accidentally hear something she shouldn't."

"Right. You're right." She glanced back at the door a few yards from her.

"Unless you want to talk inside. We can do that. It's completely up to you."

"Okay. I've cracked her bedroom door, and I'll just crack this door, too, so if she calls for me I'll hear her."

She followed him out onto the deck. The stars shined brightly again, at least those they could see through the leaves of the tree. Below them, the glow from the RV lit up the small space around the camper. Buck rested on a pallet, but his ears perked up.

He was alert.

In guard mode.

Danielle needed to talk, too, but she would wait to hear what Reece had to say. "What is it, Reece? Did you learn something that could end this? Of course, that's a stupid question. If you did, then we wouldn't still be here."

"There are a couple of things I wanted to share with you. I was working on a murder case in the park when I ran into you at the gas station. I've learned two things—the same gun was used on both the murder victim and John. And two, that John had talked to the murder victim the week before. He worked at a tech firm."

Danielle stared at him and soaked in this new information. What did it mean?

"Did John say anything to you about what he was working on?" Reece asked. "Anything at all that could help?"

"No. If he did, I would have told you."

"What about Lucy?"

"What?" She gave him an incredulous look.

Reece chuckled. "John created a password with her help. He hid his laptop in her special hiding place. I just thought maybe she knows something else that he shared."

She sighed. "I hope not, Reece. But in the morning, I'll talk to Lucy and get her talking about her uncle John. I'll listen closely. Maybe she'll spill some other secret he told her."

"Or you could simply ask her if he told her a secret."

Danielle frowned. "I really hope that's not the case. If he put her life in that kind of danger, not even counting what's already happened, I don't know if I can ever forgive him."

"I know it seems ludicrous, but I want to get you back to your safe and normal life as quickly as possible. So it's worth a try. Worth an ask."

"Safe. Normal. What is that anymore?"

Her question was the perfect transition.

Reece would be open and honest with Danielle and give her the opportunity to share any…*secrets*…she might have.

He allowed the symphony of night sounds to relax him. A warm breeze blew and pulled at a few strands of her hair. She shoved her tresses behind her ears, and to him, she looked so young to be the mother of a six year old. Danielle was as beautiful as the day he'd first met her. Even more beautiful, actually, but she was so sweet, and the love she showered on her daughter—now that was something to behold. That was true beauty.

He thought back to that moment when he first met her—she'd forgotten to put the emergency brake on and her car had rolled out of the parking lot. She started chasing it, and Reece left his sack of groceries on the ground and chased it with her. He beat her to the vehicle and hopped in and was able to stop it before it rolled out into a busy street and killed someone. When she caught up to him, she'd been breathless and filled with remorse and shame. Turned out that someone had absconded with his groceries. She offered to cook him dinner. It was the least she could do, she'd said. Brave of her given he was a stranger, but he'd mentioned his brother working in the county sheriff's department and that he was a Navy SEAL, and she relaxed in his company. They hit it off quickly. Maybe too quickly. Okay, obviously too quickly.

"What is it, Reece?"

Her question pulled him back to the present and the reason they were on this deck to talk.

"What more did you need to tell me?"

Need was a strong word. Maybe it was more that he wanted to tell her. No. Wait. He definitely needed to tell her and hoped that he wasn't being selfish.

"I… I wanted to tell you what happened to me."

"What happened to you?" She angled her head so that her hair fell like a curtain, hanging out over the deck railing.

Crickets chirped. Frogs sang. Down below them, Buck paced in front of the RV. Sniffed around. All these things Reece was aware of as he focused on Danielle.

"Yes. What happened…before."

"Oh, Reece. You don't have—"

"I want to explain. I need to explain. I hope you'll hear me out."

Danielle stared ahead into the night.

What was she thinking? He almost lost his nerve, but now was his chance to push through. Maybe in the sharing, she would open up, too.

He had to know.

"I never should have left you the way I did, and I'm sorry. I've regretted that decision ever since."

"You had no choice. You were a Navy SEAL. You had a job to do, and I knew that. I went into the whole thing with my eyes open. I don't blame you. And I don't regret my time with you for one moment. So there's nothing for you to explain. We both knew what we were doing."

How did Reece make her understand? "I had a covert mission, Danielle. Not even my family knows, so I can't tell you the specifics, but I was injured."

She tilted her head, lifting her blue eyes to him. Compassion flooded them. "I'm so sorry."

"I was in a coma."

"Like John…" Her words sounded anxious.

He nodded. "Only I was in a coma for two years."

She covered her mouth as she gasped. "Oh no. Reece. I wish I had known."

Unshed tears shimmered in her eyes. She was so beautiful, so sensitive and compassionate. He wanted to hug her to him now. But he knew better. If he cared about her at all, he knew not to open that door, even though he'd been foolish, kissing her before.

"When I woke up, I went through extensive rehab. I don't know what difference it makes now, but you need to know."

"Thank you for telling me. I still… I don't understand why you're telling me."

Here goes. Reece feared he was making a mistake, but he pressed on.

"Because all I could think after I came out of that coma four years ago was you. All I wanted to do was come back and find you. I treated you so wrong." Slept with her and then let her go. Pushed her away. "Out in the jungle, I was alone. My training kept me alive, but I found the Lord. And I regretted my actions. Telling you to move on and let go was harsh. Even so, asking you to wait for me would have been selfish as well. I never should have been with you like that. Even though I hadn't seen you in years, when I got back to the States, I wanted to find you and apologize. And I found you."

Danielle's eyes widened. "You did?"

He nodded. "Yes. I found you and saw that you had a husband and a child. Of course, I knew to let it go. I didn't want to hurt you again or cause you problems. I figured, who was I kidding, you probably never gave me another thought. I was nothing but a blip on your radar. Even if that was the case, you'd made an impact on me in those two months we spent together. I never forgot you."

And now by some crazy twist, they were together again.

Danielle searched his gaze. After everything he'd just told her, he wanted to know what she was thinking.

"Did you ever find someone special, Reece?" Her voice was soft. "A wife? A girlfriend?"

He shook his head. His turn to stare out into the darkness. Sure, he'd dated a few women, but none of them ever compared to the memory of his time with Danielle. He'd been the one who hadn't moved on, and he had no explanation.

But more than that, he didn't trust himself not to hurt someone else. "I just wanted to explain and say how sorry I am for allowing us to grow close when I knew I would walk away. I'm so sorry. Can you forgive me?"

"Oh, Reece." A tear spilled down her cheek. She reached up and cupped his cheek.

His pulse thundered. He hadn't meant to stir up romantic emotions. Not that.

"There's something I need to tell you—"

Buck's snarling growl and bark filled the night.

FIFTEEN

Fear gripped Danielle. She stared at the dog as Reece tensed and gripped her arm. The RV door burst open, and Eve hopped out, wearing a vest and holding a gun.

Reece lifted the buzzing radio.

"Buck and I will check it out." Eve's voice crackled through the radio. "You stay there."

"Get inside." Reece ushered Danielle into the house and closed the door.

A chill crawled over her. They'd been through so much already. *Lord, please let this be nothing at all.* A squirrel or a raccoon. But she didn't think Buck was the kind of dog to go nuts over forest critters.

Reece urged her deeper into the house. He looked her up and down as if to assess her.

Status: terrified. Time to redirect. "I didn't know you had radios," she said.

"You go and be with Lucy. Stay with her." He ushered her to the bedroom.

Danielle hesitated at the door. "Wait. Don't I get a radio?"

"There are only two." He gripped her shoulders and lowered his voice. "I'm not going anywhere, except onto the deck."

"Promise?"

"I might walk around the perimeter on the ground near the tree house. Now, please go be with Lucy."

Danielle nodded. What else could she do? Reece was here to do a job. To protect them both.

"Please be careful," she said.

He nodded, then chambered a round and left her. She waited until she saw him head out the door, but then he leaned back in. "Maybe you should lock this behind me."

She rushed forward and locked and bolted it. Not that it would matter if someone wanted to get to them. Their past experience meant the house would eventually explode as well. Maybe that's why Ben had selected a tree house. Still, that didn't mean the house couldn't be brought down by any means necessary. She longed to stay there and watch out the window. Watch for Reece. Watch for any potential danger. At the same time, she needed to be with Lucy.

She quietly entered the bedroom and found her little girl curled in her favorite position and sleeping soundly. Tears surged, and a sob built in her chest.

Instead of remaining with Lucy, Danielle rushed from the room. She didn't want to wake Lucy, who was sure to hear her sniffles, and maybe even a sob if it escaped. Danielle covered her mouth to hide the pain.

The dog's alerting them to danger had interrupted what she might have said to Reece. She'd almost told him about his daughter. She needed to tell him. Tonight would have been the perfect moment.

He'd opened up to explain everything. Oh, if only she could have waited for him. Somehow found him—she got the sense in his words and the emotions in his eyes that he would have wanted her. He would have wanted Lucy. They would have been a family. But there was no sense in thinking about what might have been. Tom had been Danielle's husband and a father to Lucy, and he was a good man whom she had loved dearly.

Boots clomping up the steps alerted her to Reece's return. She recognized his cadence. Feral. Protective. And swiped at the tears, swallowed the fear.

He didn't come inside like she thought but remained on the deck, pacing from the front to the side and back to the front. Standing guard.

Reece had the right to know about his daughter, but Lucy was Danielle's priority. Her entire existence revolved around caring for and protecting Lucy. Out front on the deck, Reece paused, and she watched his silhouette against the night sky.

As much as she wanted him to stay and be Lucy's father, she had to be honest with herself. Former Navy SEAL–turned–special agent Reece Bradley was still a man who could leave them behind to protect the world. Telling him that he was Lucy's father would give him permission to step into Lucy's life and then leave her crushed when he wasn't there for her.

And she couldn't do that to either of them. Best to keep her distance until this was over.

God, please let it end tonight. Please keep us safe and let this horror be over.

Gunshots resounded somewhere out there in the dark forest.

Reece dashed down the stairs. Danielle peered through the windows and spotted his form running into the woods.

See? Off to save the world.

At the moment, he was saving them, but in the future, it would be someone else.

Danielle didn't blame him. In fact, she would have urged him to go help Eve. Her heart pounded as she paced back and forth. This tree house was amazing and provided a sense of safety and security...except in a situation like this.

They were trapped. Those steps were the only way in or out. No climbing through the window or out the back door if an assailant decided to come for them. Danielle continued pacing, peering out the windows. She turned off all the lights so she could better see outside.

"Mommy?" Lucy's tiny voice called from the bedroom.

"I'm coming." She entered the room just as Lucy started running. She caught her up in her arms.

"I heard something scary. I want to go home."

"Oh, honey." Danielle held her tight. "Soon. We'll go home soon."

She squeezed her eyes shut. Maybe after tonight that's exactly what she should do. Just go home. She didn't know anything. John hadn't given them anything.

"Lucy, baby, did Uncle John ever give you something? Did he tell you a secret?"

"Oh, Mommy. I'm so sorry. I... I was scared to tell you."

Danielle tensed, anger at her brother rising. "What is it? What did he tell you?"

"Not a secret. But he gave me the heart necklace, remember? I was supposed to wear it when we came to see him, and I forgot," Lucy cried.

"Oh, Lucy. Don't cry, honey. There's nothing to cry about. Uncle John will probably get you a new necklace when he wakes up." Could the necklace Lucy had left at home hold information? Clues?

John had better come out of that coma, because Danielle was going to kill him when he woke up.

A creak somewhere in the house stilled her.

"Come on, honey, let's get you back to bed."

Another creak. Someone coming up the steps.

"Lucy, stay here, okay? I need to go check on something." She tucked Lucy under the covers.

Shutting the bedroom door, she remained along the wall and moved to peer out the window.

Just who was coming up the steps?

"Danielle, it's me." Reece knocked lightly on the front door.

She sagged with relief and rushed to unlock and unbolt the door. Reece grabbed her into a hug.

"What happened? I heard gunshots."

"Eve fired at the man. That is, well, after he shot Buck."

"Oh no!"

"Buck will be fine. Eve is rushing him to the vet."

"But the man…"

"He got away." He gripped her shoulders. "Buck warned us of an intruder, so that worked. He didn't get anywhere near you."

Danielle stepped from his grip. "Was it the same man? Or some random guy in the woods?"

"It was the man who abducted you from the campsite."

"How did he find us? I don't understand. We can't live like this, Reece. No matter where we go, someone will find us. Maybe we should just set a trap for him."

"I'm already talking to some people about putting you in a place built like a fortress."

"No. I won't live life in a prison. Lucy wants to go home."

Reece paced. "Think about Lucy and keeping her safe, Danielle."

"I am thinking about Lucy and how to end this so she'll be safe. She mentioned tonight that she had forgotten to wear the heart necklace John had given her. He had wanted her to wear that when she came to see him."

He held her gaze.

"It could be nothing," she said.

"Or it could be everything."

Reece sat next to Danielle and Lucy on the flight back to Louisville, Kentucky. He was in the aisle seat, while Lucy was in the center seat. Danielle by the window.

"Mommy what if Uncle John wakes up and we're not there to see him? What if he asks for us and we can't come? I would feel bad."

"It's okay. We're going to get your necklace—the one he gave you and asked you to wear when you saw him—and we'll come back to see him. You can make him smile when you wear your necklace. How does that sound?"

Lucy's pink lips only slightly curved as questions lingered in her blue eyes. Reece hated every bit of what was happening. He hated that Lucy had gone through so much. He wished he could do something to end this— well, at least do it faster. He was doing his best for now.

Reece shared a look with Danielle, and she bit her

bottom lip. He understood her concern. If the necklace turned out to be important—as in the bad men were after it—then Lucy couldn't wear it. But Reece had no doubt that Danielle would make her daughter understand if it came to that.

God, please let it be that simple.

Whatever information John had hidden could give them insight into who was after Danielle and Lucy. Either that or John could wake up from the coma and tell them everything.

Last night on the deck, after Reece had been transparent with her about the last few years, he'd opened the door for her to share with him. She'd been about to do just that when Buck had signaled an intruder was approaching the property. The opportunity for that conversation, whatever she might have shared, had not arisen again. Eve had texted them after rushing Buck to a local veterinarian that her guard dog for hire would be perfectly fine. The risk came with the business, she'd said.

A man had already died for whatever was sought, and one was in a coma. A key. A code. Information. Money? And until they had figured this out, Danielle and Lucy were in mortal danger.

Lucy squeezed his hand. "It's all right, Reece. I trust God, don't you?"

The words curled around his heart until he thought it might burst. His breathing quickened with the rising emotions, and he returned her squeeze. He waited until his voice would work again and he found the words. "Yes, Lucy, I trust God."

Lord, help me to have faith like a child...

The jet landed, and they grabbed their luggage at

baggage claim, along with Reece's checked firearm, then Danielle led them to her car, which she'd left in long-term parking. Reece cautioned her as he looked the red Jetta over for any obvious tampering. A GPS device or worse, a bomb, could have been planted on the car. That was, if their travel to Louisville had been anticipated.

Satisfied the car hadn't been tampered with, they loaded their few belongings in the car. Reece sat in the passenger seat while Danielle drove. He would have preferred a rental car for this particular venture in order to give them the extra layer of protection, but Danielle needed some normalcy back in her life. Lucy, too. Plus, there wasn't any sense in continuing to pay for parking. He just hoped they weren't making a big mistake.

Danielle maneuvered through the Louisville traffic and then into the suburbs.

"I don't think anyone has followed us," she said.

She didn't say what they were both thinking. Someone had found them at each of their locations, despite that he and Danielle had long ago discarded their cell phone SIM cards, still keeping their actual cells to use after this was over and life returned to normal. There was nothing else he could think. No other way they could be tracked at this point, at least that he could think of. He'd asked Anthony to look into that as well. Danielle discarded the earrings and the watch she'd been wearing.

"Are we there yet, Mommy?"

"How much farther?"

He and Lucy had asked their questions simultaneously. Reece chuckled.

"Our home is up ahead," Danielle said. "Fourth house on the right. Black shutters and a red door. It feels so strange to be coming home under these circumstances."

"We'll do our best to remedy the awkwardness, and you can feel more at home the next time you come home," Reece said. "Do me a favor. Pass by your house slowly but don't turn into the drive. Let's give the neighborhood a good, long, thorough look before we park and enter the house. There could be someone with bad intentions waiting for you there."

He rubbed the back of his neck. Now that they were actually here, he liked this idea even less. "In fact…"

"Don't say it," she said as she steered past the house she'd described. He looked it over. Took in the neighboring houses, trees and bushes, searching for someone lying in wait.

"Don't say what?" he asked.

Danielle turned at the corner and drove around the block. "I already know what you're going to say. You want to be the one to go inside the house alone and get Lucy's locket, and you want us to stay in a hotel tonight instead of my home."

"Not a bad idea," he chuckled. "Thanks for coming up with that."

She'd almost made the whole block and was near the house again. "That *is* what you were going to say, wasn't it?"

"Nope."

Danielle steered toward the house then turned into the driveway.

"I was going to say I'd like to check the house first and clear it before you two come inside."

* * *

Danielle parked the car and sighed, though she wasn't sure it was in relief. "Look, Reece, it's broad daylight. The sun is shining. It's a Saturday and the neighbors are home." She hated every bit of this. She wanted to walk into her house and feel at home and forget the last few days.

Lucy hadn't even gotten to celebrate her birthday.

"We're home, we're home, we're home. Mommy!" Lucy unbuckled. "Can I get out now? I want to see my room."

Danielle caught Reece's warning look. "Yes, we're home. But Reece is going to check the house out and make sure it's safe first, okay?" Was she crazy to come back here? Did she really believe that she could sleep in her house right now? Stay here? Considering the lengths that the men had already gone to, kidnapping her and Lucy and then blowing up two houses, Danielle wasn't so sure about anything anymore. But she definitely didn't want to lose her house.

Danielle left the car running for the moment and handed Reece the house keys. He got out of the car, and at the door, she saw him brandish his gun. She'd seen him do that many times over the last many hours they had been thrown together. He hadn't gone into the house yet and remained in the shadows of the doorway, so she couldn't see him clearly. Why wasn't he going inside? What was he waiting for?

She appreciated his thoughtfulness in keeping to the shadows, considering neighbors could be watching. In fact, her neighbor Naomi was just rounding the corner of her home. The consummate gardener, she held pansies in her gloved hands. Her eyes grew big when she spotted Danielle's car.

Oh no...

She set the flowers down, shaded her eyes then smiled and waved.

"Mommy, that's Miss Naomi. She's coming to say hi. Can we get out now?"

"I suppose we'd better." Danielle opened her door and then moved to open the back door for Lucy, who practically flew out of the vehicle and headed straight for Naomi. The woman had been Danielle's confidante and a source of encouragement over the years and especially since Tom had died, bringing cookies, casseroles and a good listening ear.

Naomi's bright smile faded. "Oh dear, what's happened?"

Danielle kept her smile in place. Naomi's question almost broke her. How could the woman tell so much? "I...um... Why do you ask?" Maybe she could stall Naomi or only give her part of the truth. She wasn't sure how much to share.

When she glanced at her house, she saw Reece marching over to her, a grim expression on his face.

She wasn't sure what that was about, but she hadn't yet told Naomi a thing. "Naomi, this is my friend Reece Bradley."

"Oh?" Naomi smiled, questions in her eyes. "Is...is everything okay? Is your brother okay?"

Naomi was far too intuitive. Danielle should have known this would happen. Reece's jaw was working. He didn't want to bring Naomi into the small circle, but he didn't understand her neighbor would be worried and it would be better to tell her the truth.

"Why don't you come on inside, and I'll tell you everything," Danielle said. She gestured toward the house, and Naomi started forward.

"Danielle." Reece's tone caused her to hesitate, and she waited for him to continue.

"I'm not sure that's a good idea."

"What's going on?" Naomi fisted her hands on her hips. "Danielle, are you in some kind of trouble? Is this man bothering you? Controlling you in some way? Should I call the police? Because I won't stand by and see you come to harm."

"No, no." Danielle pressed her hand against her forehead. Where did she even start with an explanation?

Lucy grabbed Reece's hand. "Miss Naomi, Reece is our friend. He protects us."

With Lucy's proclamation, Naomi's mouth dropped open, then slowly closed as she scrutinized Reece. "Protects you from what? From whom?"

Danielle sighed. "As I said, let's take this inside." She urged them all toward the door.

"Danielle." Reece again. He hadn't budged. "Can I have a moment with you?"

"We're all friends here," she said. "I don't have anything to hide."

His frown deepened. "The house is a wreck."

"As in, I'm a terrible housekeeper?"

He shook his head.

Reece held the door for Danielle, Lucy and Naomi. He would have strongly urged Danielle against bringing her neighbor into the danger zone by telling her everything, but Danielle had made her decision before

Reece even left the house. He saw that by the stern set
of her jaw and the defiance in her eyes.

He had no choice but to believe that Danielle could
trust this woman completely. That being the case, he
hoped and prayed danger wouldn't stalk her as well. In
the meantime, he waited for the three ladies to absorb
what they saw. He stood back and allowed Danielle and
Lucy to take in their ransacked home. The looks of horror and pain on their faces hurt him deeply. Clearly the
men stalking them had found the time to fly out here
ahead of them, or another way, as in hiring someone to
do this job and search for the wanted item in Danielle's
house. Or had the house been broken into after Danielle
and Lucy had headed for California?

Naomi held Lucy and comforted the little girl as she
whimpered. "I want to go to my room. I want to see it."

The neighbor glanced at Danielle, clearly disturbed
about the news practically falling from the sky on her
within the last few minutes.

Danielle nodded. "It's okay to go see your room."

Naomi disappeared down the hallway with Lucy. The
child loved the woman, it seemed, and that made Reece
feel more comfortable about her, but then again, Lucy
could love a lot of people who didn't deserve her love.

At least he would get a few moments alone with Danielle. "Given that the previous houses have blown up—"

"The tree house?" She eyed him, her lips pressed
in a thin line.

"Not that I know of. Still, I wouldn't advise staying
here. Let's find what we came for. That could be all we
need in terms of answers to who is behind the search."

"Or all we need in terms of luring them into a law

enforcement trap," she said. "My guess is there's a small thumb drive of some kind in that locket."

"I hope you're right. At least I think." Because if she was right, then John had endangered them. Reece didn't like to think that John could have orchestrated something so dangerous, putting the wanted item in proximity to Lucy, his precious niece. His tactics put her in unnecessary danger.

Anger surged in Danielle's eyes. Was she angry with her brother? Was she thinking the same thing as Reece? Or angry at the way her home, her life, had been invaded and ripped to shreds?

Reece hoped to do everything he could to put it back together again.

What am I thinking? He couldn't stick around that long. But he could get the people behind this and put them away.

Lucy ran down the hallway. "Mommy, Mommy. I found it! Now we can take it back to Uncle John."

Danielle crouched and caught Lucy's bouncing form.

Lucy held the necklace up so the chain hung from her fingers and the locket dangled at the bottom. "Will you put it on me? Can I wear it?"

Danielle took it from her fingers, lifted it up to look at it, then glanced at Reece, the question evident in her eyes. *What do we do with this?*

"Lucy, would you mind if I looked at your necklace first?" Reece asked. "It's so pretty and I want to see it up close."

Lucy's smile grew brilliant. "Of course. Will *you* put it on me?"

And at that moment, right then and there, Reece lost his heart to Danielle's little girl, Lucy. Maybe he'd lost it a long time ago. He tried to hide the emotions exploding inside with a simple smile.

"I can try." He gently took the necklace from Danielle and peered at it. Reece moved to the brighter light in the kitchen then looked the locket over.

"Do you like it, Reece?"

"Yes, sweetie, it's beautiful. I wonder if this locket opens."

"I don't think so." Lucy stared up at him, watching his every move.

He tried to look for a secret slot where a small thumb drive could be inserted but couldn't find it.

"Will you put it on me now?"

"Sure thing."

She lifted her hair up. He moved to stand behind Lucy and tried again to open the locket one last time, or see if he missed a slot where a drive was hidden. Nothing.

"What's the matter?" Lucy angled to look at him. "Can't you get it to work?"

Danielle squatted to look Lucy in the eyes. "Honey, I'm thinking that after our long day of travel, you might like to take a bubble bath and get cleaned up. Get into some clean clothes. We can put the locket on later. Or wait until the morning." Danielle's singsong tone was meant to appease Lucy.

Lucy stuck out her bottom lip. "I want to wear it now."

"Now, Lucy," Naomi said. "Your mother is right. In fact, I'm thinking you might prefer to stay at my house tonight until we can get this mess cleaned up. What do you think?"

Danielle glanced up at Naomi, appreciation in her eyes. "Thank you."

"Plus, the police need to look the place over. Gather evidence." Reece got on his cell to call them. He'd cleared the place, and Danielle and Lucy had needed to see it and look for the necklace, but now they had recovered the necklace, they were stepping all over the crime scene.

At Danielle's questioning look, he said, "This needs to be reported and part of the narrative. They could find fingerprints, too." He must be losing his touch not to have already called the authorities, but at the thought of finding the necklace, something potentially linked to his investigation, he'd zeroed in on finding what John had hidden, and only now thought of calling the police. This situation had weighed on him, especially with the two dear-to-his-heart ladies who were in danger.

While he was on his cell, giving the information to the local police, he partially listened to Danielle speaking with Naomi. She held Lucy in her arms so she wouldn't run off somewhere in the house. The necklace around her neck, Lucy peered at the locket.

"We wouldn't want to impose on you," Danielle said.

"Nonsense. I want you to stay. I've missed you. I'm worried about you."

Danielle held Reece's gaze as she said the next words to Naomi. "You could be in danger if we stay there. I need to talk to Reece about it and get his okay. Like Lucy said, he's protecting us. He's investigating, try-ing to solve this, while he's protecting us. I'll explain everything later, okay?"

Naomi hugged herself, clearly disturbed by every-thing happening to Danielle. "You and this Reece fel-low, you seem…close."

Danielle's cheeks reddened. Reece couldn't help notice that Naomi was taking it all in. A very perceptive woman.

"We've known each other a long time," Danielle said.

Naomi's gaze flicked to Reece then down to Lucy. "How long have you known him, dear?"

SIXTEEN

Danielle tucked Lucy into the guest bedroom at Naomi's house, right next door to the home she'd shared with Tom. Staying here seemed surreal and served to emphasize how precarious and dangerous their situation was. At least Naomi's home was warm and friendly, and you could feel the sense of love. The room was painted lavender and smelled of vanilla. The twin beds were covered in beautiful lavender and yellow quilts. She breathed in the smell of a loving home. Of safety and security, and wished it could be so. Naomi had served them a roast she'd already had cooking and thanked the Lord for making sure she was prepared for her guests.

"Mommy, I don't want to sleep here. I want to sleep in my own bed."

"I know, honey. But you understand that we've had bad men chasing us."

Lucy yawned as she nodded. "And Reece is protecting us. Is that why we can't stay at home?"

"Yes, my darling." Danielle swept her hand over Lucy's temple. "You've been so, so brave through it all. It's almost over, though, so I just need you to be brave and strong little longer."

"Then will we go back to see Uncle John? I want him to wake up and see my necklace."

Danielle smiled and kissed her daughter on her forehead. "I can't make promises right now, Lucy."

"I understand. You always say don't make promises you can't keep. Let your yea be a yea and your nay be a nay. Like the Bible says. But I've never heard you say yea or nay. You only say yes or no."

Danielle chuckled, and at Lucy's reference to the Bible, her gaze snagged on Naomi's leather-bound Bible resting on the side table. She knew that particular burgundy Bible was one of many Bibles Naomi owned. She liked to have different translations and different Bible covers.

"Tell you what. I need to go out and talk to Naomi and Reece for a few minutes. I'll try to sneak away from them so I can come to bed early. Maybe I'll read the Bible to you then. How about that?"

Lucy nodded and rested her head on the pillow, her gaze taking in the peaceful landscape paintings on the walls—one painting even depicting a field of lavender. The soothing room reminded her of her neighbor, whose very presence was calming.

Danielle left a dimly lit lamp on in the room and left the door partially cracked. Lucy blinked, her lids heavy. She would probably be dreaming by the time Danielle came back. She would prefer just to curl up next to her and read the Bible, but she needed to chat with Naomi and Reece.

Danielle headed down the short hallway to the kitchen. Reece was just tucking his cell phone away, and he approached the kitchen nook as Naomi set cups out on the table and poured tea.

He saw Danielle and smiled. "I don't anticipate any trouble tonight. Your house is blocked off as a crime scene connected to my ongoing investigation. I need to head over and talk to the investigator who is still there. Are you okay with that?"

She nodded. "Yes. Sure. Anything to make this go faster. Did you tell him about…about the explosions?"

"Explosions?" Naomi's hands shook and rattled the cups. "What explosions?"

Danielle sighed. "Maybe I should have told you everything before you let us stay."

"You're like my daughter," Naomi said. "You can stay no matter what, but I would like to know about the explosions."

Reece nodded for Danielle to go ahead and share. Naomi had brought them into her home. She needed to know.

"Two of the houses where we were tracked blew up." Danielle hated the sound of those words.

Naomi set her cup on the table, her hand trembling. She pressed the other shaking hand to her mouth. Unshed tears formed in her eyes.

Danielle looked to Reece. "You should go meet with the police. I'll be here. Naomi and I can comfort each other."

"Are you sure?" His eyes pierced through her, searching for the truth.

"I'm as sure as I'll ever be." There. The truth. And nothing but the truth.

Reece gave his familiar cursory nod. It was settled, then. "I won't be long."

Danielle slipped into a chair at the table and hoped Naomi would follow her lead. She couldn't leave Naomi until she told her the whole sordid story, and she wished she hadn't told Lucy that she would come back to the bedroom soon. This looked to be a very long night, when all she wanted to do was curl up in bed, knowing she and Lucy were safe, at least for one night.

Danielle inhaled a long breath and shared the events of the last couple of days, starting with her arrival in California. Naomi listened in silence, sometimes staring at her teacup, other times looking directly at Danielle. But always with deep frown lines in her forehead and concern in her eyes.

"And all that brought us home, and you know the rest. Now we're here in your home. Maybe bringing danger to you." She pressed her hand over Naomi's on the table. "I don't want to burden you with this. We'll leave tomorrow." To go where, she wasn't sure.

"Don't you dare." Naomi's fire-filled tone revealed her convictions. "You're welcome to stay right here until the danger passes and these men are put away. Let me be clear, I wouldn't want you staying alone in your own home until this is over. I think of you as family, dear. And I hope you return the sentiment."

Danielle hung her head. She didn't know what to say to that. Finally, words came to her. "You have no idea just how much your words mean to me. Just knowing that we have someone." Ever since Tom had died, it was just Danielle and Lucy—with John so far away— and yes, Naomi had been a supportive friend, but the woman was taking it a step farther.

Danielle covered a yawn and then smiled. "Sorry."

"It's okay. You must be exhausted. I appreciate you sharing everything with me so now I know how to pray and what to be on the lookout for. Why don't you head on to bed? Sleep late and I'll make you and Lucy breakfast when you wake, whatever time that is."

"Oh, Naomi. You're so good to us. I didn't mean to burden you with—"

"Really. It's no burden. I'd do anything for you and Lucy." Naomi rose from her chair, then pushed it back to the table.

Danielle followed her lead and took the teacups to the sink to rinse out. "You've done that and more than you'll ever know."

Naomi sighed and had that look about her—she had something delicate to say. "Reece… Does…does he know, dear?"

Danielle tensed at her words. How could Naomi know? "I… I don't understand. Know what?"

Naomi pursed her lips. "It's okay. I shouldn't pry. See you in the morning." She turned to head down the hallway.

"Naomi, wait," Danielle said. The pain of tears filled her throat. "I… How did you know?"

Naomi's sweet, tender smile filled her face. Compassion filled her eyes. "It's oh so obvious. Why, she looks just like him."

Instead of Tom. Danielle and Tom had married days before Lucy was born. Tom had moved them to Kentucky for his job, into the house right next to Naomi, who'd invited her to church. Danielle thought her heart would break.

Shame filled her, and she hung her head. "No, he doesn't know. I haven't found the right time or place to tell him in…in all this."

Naomi patted her hand. "You will, Danielle. God will show you the time and the way. But Reece might have already figured it out and is simply waiting for you to share that with him, if you so choose. He's a good man, Danielle. I can sense that right off."

"Thank you, Naomi." Danielle nodded, searching for more words, but she couldn't find them. "I should go check in on Lucy and go to bed, too." She offered her friend a smile and headed for Lucy's room.

The door was shut. She had been sure she left it cracked. Danielle opened the door to find even the small lamp on the side table turned off.

Lucy wasn't in her bed, and the window was open.

Reece finished up his conversation with the local detective. The lights were on at Danielle's house. After the house had been checked for explosives, a team had gone in and now searched for evidence, fingerprints or other DNA evidence—they desperately needed a hit to find the men after Danielle and Lucy. One or both, he didn't know. He doubted the techs would find fingerprints, but maybe the intruder had left DNA evidence. Law enforcement cracked cases because criminals made mistakes, and Reece was hoping for that mistake. This break-in could be the very break they'd needed. Now that he thought about it, maybe that's why the last two houses had been blown up—the guy wanted to cover his tracks completely. No DNA evidence would be left behind in a fire. A really over-the-top way to go about it, to Reece's way of thinking, but then again, this guy could be a mercenary or someone with nothing to lose. Or didn't care.

Reece's cell buzzed.

Anthony. Reece replied as he walked back toward Naomi's home.

"What have you got?"

"Two things. The image you sent me that Lucy took on the cell phone paid off. The man who followed her is Johan Umber. He's a hired assassin. A mercenary. Used to be a bomb specialist. Add to that, bombers sometimes have signatures, as in a certain way they construct bombs. The elements gathered from the two houses confirmed this was his work. So we have a BOLO out on him."

"Good work. You said you had two things?"

"Yes, and this is equally important, if not more. I figured out how Danielle and Lucy have been tracked."

His whole body tensed as he stared at Naomi's house. "Well? What is it?"

"I discovered intel on John's laptop regarding Lucy's pacemaker. It has some interesting features. I did some additional research and found that only a few of its kind were made."

"What are you saying, exactly?"

"I'm saying that someone with know-how could track her through her pacemaker."

Reece scratched his head. "How is that possible?"

"She has a cloud-connected medical device, which is continually monitored, so it's not a stretch to go that next step."

Fear gripped his insides and twisted. "I need to go. See if there's anything we can do about stopping that from happening. If we can't fix that, it will mean we never get her somewhere safe. She'll need…special protection." Or to end this once and for all. "We have to find whoever is behind this. Find the bomb-crazy mercenary, too, and find out who hired him and why."

"I hear you," Anthony said. "I'm working the medical device piece, but honestly, I don't know that we can simply turn it off without risking her life. I need to figure out how this was done. Someone with specific expertise was on this."

"Greg Lewis." Reece rubbed his temple.

"Who is Greg Lewis?"

"He was the software guy that John Steele met with a week before they were both shot. Greg was killed. I don't know if he has any connection to this, but maybe John wanted Lucy monitored and followed. I have no idea why. I'm pulling that out of my tactical hat."

"Well, at the very least, we can check on it. I'll look at your reports to find where he worked."

"I know it was a software firm in San Francisco."

"This could tell us something."

"Or his connection with John could have nothing to do with tracking Lucy."

Reece sighed… This situation was far worse than he could have dreamed. He loved that little girl. *God, please don't let anything happen to her.* "You did good, Anthony. Keep me informed."

He ended the call and sprinted to the house. Gently opened the door. The home was quiet.

Naomi was in the kitchen pouring milk.

"Where's Danielle?" He whispered the question.

"She's in bed already. Lucy, too, of course. What's wrong?"

Reece breathed a sigh of relief, but concern for their safety wouldn't let him rest. He strode quickly down the hallway and listened at the door. Should he disturb Danielle's sleep to tell her the news?

He rubbed his forehead. He didn't know what to do.

Naomi touched his arm and motioned for him to follow her. He didn't have time for this, but then again…

He followed her into the living room and waited.

"Tell me what's going on and how I can help."

He scraped his hand through his hair. "I wish you could, Naomi. This is just…" What was it about this woman that made him want to bare it all? He got why Danielle so easily trusted her.

Reece shared the news he'd just learned. Naomi listened intently. Her mouth moved as she paced the room. Praying? Reece liked this woman even more.

"I think I should check on Danielle," she said. "Let her know… I could do it quietly and not wake Lucy up."

A wry grin lifted half his cheek. She thought he would wake up the house, he guessed.

"But then, even if she knows, what then?" Naomi asked. "Where will you go to keep Lucy safe?"

He eased onto the sofa and pressed his face into his hands. *God, she's right. What do we do next?*

He'd never imagined finding himself in this situation. He rose from the sofa and faced Naomi. "I don't know, but I think Danielle would want to know this information right away. She wouldn't want me to keep this from her."

"I agree. Do you want me to be the one to wake her then?"

"Please. Then we can decide what to do."

While Naomi went to get Danielle, Reece texted his superior about the latest developments. He felt like he was fighting an invisible monster and failing.

Naomi yelped. Cried out for him.

His heart pounded as he rushed down the hallway. Caught her as she ran from the room.

"They're gone. Danielle and Lucy are gone."

SEVENTEEN

Heart pounding, pulse roaring in her ears, Danielle drove the vehicle along the lonely two-lane road, her moisture-slick hands trembling as she clung to the steering wheel.

Terror for her little girl gripped her. Acid rose in her throat—what must Lucy be feeling and thinking?

Her heart...

Oh God, please, please keep her safe and calm. Please help her to trust in You, even though I know she must be scared.

Lucy had always had so much faith.

When Danielle returned to the bedroom and found Lucy gone, she'd spotted the note on the pillow. Printed instructions for her to follow.

Come alone or you'll never see your daughter again. You have the information whether you realize it or not. I'm running out of time. Elude your protectors. Tell them nothing. I've planted cameras and I will know your every move. Leave your cell phone behind. You'll find a silver Buick sedan parked two streets over. The key's in the wheel well. Your destination is already programmed into the GPS.

Danielle swiped at the tears as she followed the GPS instructions. She'd had no choice.

No choice!

She'd wanted to inform Reece. Leave him a note. Something. But the man had warned she would never see Lucy again. That he had cameras everywhere. She didn't know how that could be possible and had glanced around the bedroom. But she realized the search would be futile. If he had planted cameras in this room, in Naomi's house, then he would see her looking, and no matter what, she could not risk Lucy's life.

Getting Lucy back was her priority.

So she'd left no note for Reece. No information for him.

She'd been too scared to think straight. With her daughter's life on the line, following the man's intimidating instructions seemed the only path to retrieve Lucy.

But now…

Regrets accosted her. Maybe she could have left a clue. A trail. Something.

Oh God, why didn't I tell him?

But not even that mattered anymore.

Lord, help me to find Lucy. Help me to free her and keep her safe.

Tears continued to stream down her cheeks and blur her vision as she drove. She furiously swiped at them, to no avail. They just kept coming. But she was determined not to fall apart. She inhaled a deep breath and wiped at the tears one more time.

Yes. She was so done falling apart. She had to be strong. For Lucy. She had to win. This was all on her, and she couldn't think about Reece or hope that he would find them. She was on her own.

She thought if Lucy was here with her, she would encourage Danielle that God was with them and to not be afraid. An incredulous chuckle escaped. Lucy was right. God was with them both, and Danielle would try to remember that as she walked through this valley of fear and dread.

Uncertainty crawled over her. She didn't know what to expect, what would come next. Her life was not her own at the moment. The man hunting them and finding them every place—he was the man in control. He had found a way to get to them…using Lucy to draw Danielle away from Reece.

She didn't need Reece to save the day. They had lived on their own for two years since Tom's death. Though she admitted that was different. During that time, their lives had not been threatened.

Okay. Maybe…maybe she would pray for help from Reece. After all, throughout all this, she had believed God had sent Reece to protect them.

Lord, please help Reece to find us!

She parked the car at the bus station.

Now what?

Oh, she didn't like this. Not one bit.

Danielle twisted around in the car, looking to see if she could spot the man. If it was one of the two men she'd encountered before, she would recognize him. She hoped to spot Lucy somewhere.

Her heart ached to see her sweet daughter. To hold her in her arms and never let her go. This whole thing was just crazy. Why had she left her daughter for even one moment? She should have stayed with her and read the Bible to her. Emotion grew thick in her throat.

No time for what-ifs. She had to remain strong and

not let this man intimidate her. It was two thirty in the morning.

Okay. I'm here. Now what? Where are you?

She had to save her daughter at all costs.

In the rearview mirror, a figure approached from behind. Her heart pounded. This was it. A man tapped on the car window. She lowered it, and looked up into the face of the man who had come for them on multiple occasions, but not the man who had abducted them from the campground.

He'd tried to kill them, too. She didn't understand that, and here she was playing into his hands. For Lucy. She had to get her back. She was confused about whether he wanted them dead, but right now, it would seem he wanted her alive.

"Look, I told you I don't know what you're looking for. Please, please, let my little girl go."

"Get out of the car." He opened the door.

If she wanted to see Lucy, she had no choice. "Where is my daughter?"

"Follow me."

She followed him, hiking down a trail away from the station. Fear slithered around her throat and squeezed. She could be walking to her death.

Lucy could already be dead.

Oh God, please help us. "Yea, though I walk through the valley of the shadow of death, I will fear no evil: for thou art with me; thy rod and thy staff they comfort me."

I will fear no evil. I will fear no evil.

She repeated the verse over and over, hoping peace would eventually flood her soul.

The man stopped at a van. One of those big white vehicles with no windows. He slid the door open. "Get in."

"But—"

"Lucy's inside."

At that moment, Danielle felt like a little child being lured by a predator with a puppy. But this was Lucy, not a puppy, and Danielle would do what she was told, whatever that was, to get Lucy back.

The man followed her into the dimly illuminated small space. Lucy was sleeping on the dirty floor.

"Lucy!" Danielle lifted her daughter into her arms. She didn't wake up. "You...you drugged her?"

"Shut up and put on the wigs." The man's voice was gruff, unforgiving. "Change into these clothes."

"What? Why?"

"I need you to be disguised."

"You tried to kill us before. I don't understand... why disguises?"

He scratched his chin. "I never tried to kill you. I tried to get my hands on you for the intel you possess."

"What about all the shooting at the house?"

He huffed. "I needed to take your protector out to get to you."

"But you blew up those houses."

He shrugged. "That's the best part. Plus, I don't have to worry about a strand of hair, a small DNA particle left behind."

"You're crazy," Danielle said.

"And you're dumber than you look, you know that? Now, I'm ordered to deliver you."

Danielle bit back an equally accusing retort. This wasn't the time to argue with him. Danielle glanced around the van. Was there an escape? A way to get out of this now that she had Lucy?

He tugged a gun from his pocket and chambered a

round. "Just to be sure you know, I don't need the little girl."

Danielle swallowed the knot swelling against her throat.

His eyes were cold as he stared at her. "Do you understand?"

"Yes." She nodded. She had no choice but to comply.

Danielle slipped on the required hoodie. Put on a dark brown wig and glasses. She gently put a smaller dark brown wig on Lucy while she still slept, and a black hoodie. Hiding Lucy's blond curls went a long way in changing her appearance.

Danielle held Lucy again. "Okay. Now what?"

"I'll carry our sleeping 'daughter' as we get on the bus."

"We're riding a bus?"

"Just to get to the train. They won't consider a passenger train, and even if they do, they're not looking for a family." He tugged on a baseball cap and a jean jacket, both transforming him to an everyday guy.

Danielle hoped that facial recognition software was in place somewhere that could help them to be located.

They boarded the bus. "Just how far are we going?"

"Shut up."

Danielle held Lucy on the bus ride, their captor sitting in the aisle seat. He never let her forget his threat on Lucy—and that would keep her compliant. The ride seemed to take forever, but finally Danielle drifted off into a restless sleep in the uncomfortable seat next to a dangerous man. Once they arrived in Chicago, they walked four blocks from the bus station to the train station. He carried Lucy the whole way. Danielle remained close by his side. She felt weak and powerless to do anything more than comply with his demands.

On the train, he closed the door of a private compartment behind them. Lucy stirred, her eyes wide with fear, then they grew wider when she took in Danielle. "Mommy!"

Lucy pressed her face into Danielle's shoulder.

"Shh. It's okay, honey," Danielle said. "It's going to be all right."

"It's not going to be okay, Mommy. The bad man got us. The bad man has us."

He pulled out a syringe. "Keep her quiet or I'll have to put her to sleep again."

The panic that had gripped her tightened. "I don't know what's in that syringe, but that could be dangerous to Lucy. Please, give me a few moments. I'll get her to be quiet, I promise."

She gripped Lucy's arm. "Shh, honey. Remember when you told Reece that everything was going to be okay and he just needed to trust God?"

Lucy's big blue eyes teared up as she nodded.

"That's what I want you to do right now. God will never leave you nor forsake you."

Lucy nodded again, but the crease in her forehead and the confusion in her eyes could break Danielle's heart. "I want you to rest and be calm. It isn't good for you to get upset. Just rest here in my arms. Mommy's got you. God has got you."

Lucy snuggled against Danielle. *Oh God, please be here for my Lucy. Let her know that she can trust You.*

And Danielle. She struggled to have faith in this situation. She wasn't scared for herself or for her life but for Lucy. If anything happened to Lucy…

She lifted her face. The man remained standing at the door like a sentinel as if he contemplated putting her and Lucy both to sleep with a syringe or two.

"If I do everything you say and I help you find what you want, I want your promise that you'll let Lucy go. She has a heart condition. An implanted medical device."

The way the man looked at her, she got the distinct impression the information she'd shared about Lucy's pacemaker was no surprise to him. Then, suddenly, his eyes widened as he looked from Danielle and to Lucy, staring at her daughter with new interest that kindled terror in Danielle's gut.

As the train started moving, he took a seat opposite them, his eyes never leaving Lucy's form. "I think I know where your brother hid the information. Now it's just a matter of how to get to it."

A new fear crawled over her.

Reece peered out of the helicopter and studied the terrain below them, wishing he could simply jump on the moving passenger train. As it was, they would be cutting it close to make the station before the train stopped.

It had taken him precious time to get a warrant for the company that collected the data from Lucy's device via the cloud in his search for her. They needed someone with know-how so they could also track her, too, but time was running out.

They only reason they were following the train was because a neighbor had seen Danielle get into that car, and they had tracked the vehicle to the bus station. The only bus leaving at three in the morning was headed to

Chicago. Security cameras took images of a family—
a man carrying a child and a woman—getting on the
train in Chicago.

A closer look, and Reece knew he was looking at
a disguised Danielle and Lucy. Umber was also disguised, but recognizable. Since his previous tactics
hadn't worked, he'd switched things up at Naomi's
house, using Lucy to lure Danielle to him. But finding
them had taken far too much time. Reece had to get on
that train and get to them first, grab them at the first
stop out of Chicago. They could be herded off the train
at any of the thirty-three stops between Chicago and
San Francisco and be missed. Another reason he wanted
to get on the train first was that if the train stopped and
law enforcement rushed on, the abductor could flee
again alone, take them with him or take their lives.

Any way he looked at it, the risk was much too great.

He would get on the train first and get to them. He'd
notified the railroad police agency, who would contact
SWAT to assist in taking down the abductor—Johan
Umber, a hired assassin. This time Umber hadn't been
hired as an assassin only but rather a delivery man hired
to secure information *before* the kill, and then he blew
things up for thrills per his expertise.

Reece was just about to speak to the pilot about in-
creasing speed when he noticed they had passed the
train and could land near the train station ahead of the
train. The helicopter landed in a parking lot, and Reece
hopped onto the ground. He ducked to avoid the rotors
and ran away from the rotor wash and noise, toward
the train station.

He flashed his credentials as he went and finally
met up with the train station police and the SWAT team

captain, Sparky Reeves, who explained he would have men on all the train exits.

"I don't want him spooked. Do you understand? There's a little girl with a heart condition on that train. I need to go in first and secure their safety."

"I understand. I'll follow the protocols as necessary."

"Then wait to hear from me before you rush him. I'll try to isolate them in the car."

The only three-person families who had booked on the California Zephyr were in two different cars. He tugged on his hoodie to disguise himself as well. He would be boarding here. Two of the families were stopping here and getting off the train; that meant one family was staying.

He couldn't know which of them would be *his* family. *His* family?

Anthony had been researching the booked travelers to try and identify which family would include Danielle and Lucy, but Reece couldn't wait on the information. He had to act now.

"Your men have the pictures of them, right? They could have switched their disguises again, but it isn't likely."

"We'll do our best."

The train slowed at the station for passengers to disembark.

God, please help me find them.

He climbed onto one of the cars, pushing past a few passengers getting off and beating those getting on, and made his way, hoodie pulled up, to one of the cars holding the family in the demographic he needed. He would check every single car if he had to. His gun was hidden away and easy to reach. A family of three pushed past—but not the one he was looking for. He walked through the dining car that separated two of the cars he needed to board.

In his earpiece, Captain Reeves spoke. "Two families exited. They do not match descriptions."

The thing was, this Johan Umber could very well exit the train with or without travel plans. He could switch it up on them if he spotted anything suspicious.

One SWAT guy leaning out, stepping out of line too quickly, could tip Umber off.

On the next car after the dining car, Reece neared the quarters where Danielle and Lucy could be kept. This was the last one. He pressed his back against the wall next to the door and listened. Was it possible to hear their conversation inside?

What did he do now? Just wait on them to leave? Or barge in, risking their lives?

No matter how he looked at it, any action he chose could be a risk to them. But inaction was the biggest risk of all.

The pocket door slid open.

He tensed. Ready to shoot.

A man stepped out. Not Umber, like he expected. Reece pointed his weapon. "Where are they?"

"I don't know what you're talking about, man."

"Keep your hands in the air. Get back into your quarters."

The man did as he was told. Reece pushed into the space with him and found it empty.

"Why are you here? A man, woman and child were booked for this space."

The man still held his hands high, and sweat beaded on his brow. "Look, I thought it was weird. Some guy paid me a couple of hundred bucks. Said there was a smell in here that was making his little girl sick, so he asked if we could trade. I didn't smell anything, so I said sure." He shrugged. "I haven't committed a crime."

Could Reece believe him?

"Okay, which car, which room, did you trade with him? Tell me."

The man gestured to the left. "Three doors down."

"Stay here. Stay right here. I might need to come back for you." Reece flashed his credentials. "If you leave without permission, I'll find you and you'll be sorry."

"Look, man, I was leaving. I'm getting off here." The train started moving. "And now you're making me miss it."

"Let me see some ID."

The man tugged out his wallet. Reece took a picture of it. "Okay, go."

He watched the man go then ran down the three doors. He relayed what had happened to Captain Reeves.

"The train is moving. I can speak with the conductor about holding," Reeves said.

"No," Reece said. "That would signal there's an issue. I want Danielle and Lucy safe. I don't want our man to know we're tracking him."

The train kept moving. "I'll connect with law enforcement at the next stop."

Reece feared too much activity would stir the curious and some news station would end up blasting their chase on the news—and Umber would read about it on his device.

He was running out of time to save them.

EIGHTEEN

The train was heading west out of Chicago, and that's all she knew. She didn't know their final destination, but she knew this particular ride could take them all the way to California, and that would make sense. Except that if authorities had figured out they were on a train, then California would be a suspected destination. She doubted the man would take them all the way.

They'd stopped at the first station outside Chicago, and then within ten minutes continued on. Danielle considered every possible scenario for escape. The train could stop thirty-plus times before reaching California. At which of those stops would she have an opportunity to snatch Lucy and escape this man's grip? At some point, he would have to use the facilities. Would he drug them with his syringe before that?

"Where are you taking us?" she asked again. Not that she expected an answer.

The man stared at his tablet, his eyes narrowed. He didn't bother responding. No surprise there. She'd kept Lucy snuggled against her, resting, and hadn't wanted to antagonize the man so he would use his syringe on either of them. But if she could get even one answer out of him, that would be something.

As the train moved, she peered at the window and watch the sun rise higher and the terrain shift from city to suburbs to country. Farms. Wheat and corn and soy fields.

She hadn't expected him to keep them on the train too long, because eventually someone would figure out where they were, wouldn't they? But no one had so far, and her hopes continued to dive. Tears surged behind her eyes, but she held them back. She didn't want to upset Lucy even more. Keeping herself calm so she could keep Lucy calm was her priority…well, that and somehow escaping. But they had to survive until the moment for their escape arrived.

Lucy finally stirred and rubbed her eyes. Danielle hated that her little girl was waking up to an unpleasant experience all over again.

"Mommy, I'm hungry."

Danielle glared at the man. "Well? Are you going to starve us to death?"

His eyes flicked to her then back to the tablet. "You're not going to starve."

"Listen, my little girl needs sustenance. She needs nourishment. Food."

"I know what sustenance and nourishment means. You don't need to keep talking. I could put her to sleep again and she wouldn't have to suffer with hunger."

"No, no, Mommy, no," Lucy whimpered and curled deeper into Danielle, who held her tightly. Her arms and legs had long ago gone numb from holding Lucy.

"You're a monster. You know that?"

"So I've been told."

"Can't we at least get something to drink?"

He rubbed his eyes. Maybe he hadn't fully thought this through or realized it wouldn't be so easy.

"Here's what's going to happen. We're getting off at the next stop. You can wait that long."

"Well, how long is that?"

"Not long."

"You're taking us to meet someone, aren't you? You're not the person behind this."

He reached over and yanked Lucy from Danielle's arms faster than she could have imagined. She never would have thought Lucy could be removed from her grip. Lucy screamed, and he pulled his gun out and put it under her chin.

"No, Lucy, please, baby, stop. Be quiet. It's going to be okay." Tears belied her words. "Look at me, Lucy. Look at me, my baby."

Lucy squeezed her eyes shut and curled into a ball as much as was possible while the guy held her.

"Look at me, Lucy."

Lucy slowly opened her eyes and barely turned her head.

"That's it, baby. Look at Mommy. Remember, God is with us. Even in the valley, He's here with us even now."

Instead of handing Lucy back, he gripped her tighter.

"No more talking, or I shoot you and take her." He held her gaze. "That's right. I want her now. I don't need you."

Danielle looked at the man holding her precious Lucy, horror filling her soul as she digested his words. If he killed Danielle, what would happen to her daughter? She could no longer hold the tears back, and they surged form her eyes and down her cheeks without restraint.

She didn't fear for her own life, but for Lucy.

"No…please." She bit her lip, wet with tears. "You don't understand. She can't—"

Someone knocked on the door, interrupting Danielle. "Everything all right in there? I heard someone scream."

The man's dead eyes bored into her, filling her with terror.

"Everything's fine," he said.

"Can I get you anything? Drinks? Food?"

"Water," Lucy cried out. "And I'm hungry."

Danielle's heart jackhammered. What would the man do now? The way he stared at Lucy, Danielle thought the man would hit her. At the very least he was about to drug her again.

"Please, let me hold her again. Please." She couldn't stand the sight of him holding her. The terror that must be ripping through Lucy. "She can't take it. Her heart…"

In one brisk move, he stood at the door and lowered Lucy to stand next to him against the wall. He held a clump of her hair. Gun behind his back, he gave Danielle a warning look. She pressed into the corner and pushed as far as she could from him.

If she could just get Lucy again… *I won't ever let you go again, Lucy.*

But she feared saying the words out loud.

The man slid the pocket door opened. "What—"

"Put your hands in the air or I'll shoot."

Reece!

"I don't think so, mate."

The man snatched Lucy in front of him and held the gun to her head.

Fear curdled in his gut. Beautiful, sweet Lucy's big blue eyes filled with terror. Rage overwhelmed the fear

and built in his chest. Reece had never wanted to be
in this position. This was exactly what he'd wanted to
avoid, but it couldn't be helped. And he'd forced Umber's hand—and now he could take Lucy's life right
before Reece and Danielle's eyes.

"Now, *you* put the gun down," Umber growled.

Lucy cried out as the man pressed the nine-milli-
meter muzzle harder against her head. Her blue eyes
pleaded with Reece—the man she had once believed
protected her—and he saw the hope mingled with the
fear in her gaze. She *still* believed he would protect her,
save her and her mother.

But he also took in the look of horror on Danielle's
face. Reece had never imagined he would walk right
up and snatch them away from this man's grip. Deep
inside he'd known that saving them would come to this
moment—to this sacrifice. All he had needed was to
make it to Umber's lair, where he kept those Reece trea-
sured above all else. And he was here now.

"Lower your gun!" the man shouted.

Reece lowered it. He didn't believe for a minute
Umber would shoot him here on the train and draw attention to himself and his kidnapping victims. At least
not yet.

Lucy opened her mouth wide and chomped on the
man's hand. He yelped. Her action gave Reece the distraction he needed to grip the man's gun hand to remove
the piece from him, but he was strong and still hadn't
released the gun. Still he couldn't hold the gun and
Lucy, too, especially since she continued to bite him.

Danielle reached for her and gently tried to extricate
Lucy from the dangerous man. "Let go, Lucy!"

Lucy released her bite, and the man kicked Reece's gun, sending his weapon across the room.

"Run, Danielle." Reece forced the words through gritted teeth. "Get. Out. Get. Her. Out."

He and Umber both battled for Umber's gun now.

"I can get your gun, Reece."

"No. Get out." He didn't want Danielle to stay behind and try to get it. Someone could get shot accidentally. Nor would he allow them to remain in the man's presence on the chance he had the opportunity to abduct them again. "Get her out of here."

No matter what else happened, he wanted Danielle and Lucy safe and sound—away from this killer.

"Mommy, no!" Lucy called out as Danielle carried her out of the room. "Help! Someone help us!"

The gun slipped from his hands, and he kicked it away to slide across the room. The man punched Reece, who also got a punch in. Before Reece could dive for the gun, Umber got a lock on Reece's neck to cut off his air. Reece elbowed and headbutted him. He twisted around and scrambled for the gun that had fallen under one of the beds.

Come on, come on, come on. Darkness started edging his vision. He had to win or else Danielle and Lucy would remain in danger. He stretched toward the gun at the same time he tried to break free from Umber's grip.

But Umber—a bigger man with longer arms—got Reece's gun first. Reece could breathe now but fought Umber for his own gun. As they gnashed teeth and grunted, holding the gun between them, it was just a matter of who was the stronger man now. Reece knew he didn't fit that bill and hoped that brains would win over brawn. Reece gritted his teeth, his muscles screaming as he pushed the weapon away from aiming point-blank at him. But Umber pushed the gun back toward Reece.

God, please help me. I want to have faith like a child, faith like Lucy. If I don't win this battle, their lives are at stake. They're still in trouble.

"Who. Hired. You." Reece ground each word out. He counted on being the winner, but as for the outcome, someone was going to die. He needed information before it was too late.

The gun fired, resounding in his ears and the too-close quarters.

Fire lit through him.

Oh no…

The man scrambled to his feet. Reece covered his side with his hand and watched the blood gush through.

Umber stared down at Reece. He looked at his bloody hand where Lucy had bit him. "You can die knowing that I'm going to get her. I'm going to hurt her real good."

Terror forged with anger and resolve. Reece kicked out with his leg. The man fell back, and the weapon fired into the ceiling. Reece climbed on top of him and landed a lethal blow to his throat, crushing his trachea.

Stunned, suffocating, Umber stared up at him. Their roles had shifted. Reece relieved Umber of his weapon. He glanced at the gunshot wound. A deep graze—lots of bleeding that he needed to stop or he could potentially bleed out—but he would live as long as he got to it. He wouldn't do that until he had answers while he had the chance. This guy had been working for someone. For all Reece knew, that someone was on this train.

That thought hadn't occurred to him until this moment. His cell buzzed.

"Reece, tell me what's happening." His supervisor's timing couldn't have been better. Or was that worse?

Reece glanced at Umber again and saw his eyes were now lifeless. "Umber is dead. Get someone here as soon as possible." Reece relayed the necessary information.

"And the girls?"

Reece gasped for breath and hesitated as pain spiked through him. "Somewhere on this train."

"Find them. We just learned that Jamie Blackwell, the president of AlphaGentronics, is on that train as well. We found the body of her husband, Tim Blackwell, in an alley, and based on a couple of witnesses at the campsite, he matches the description of the man who took Lucy and Danielle. We're gathering evidence on Jamie and believe she killed her husband. She could be armed and dangerous."

"Then they're still in danger," Reece said. "Get the conductor to stop the train before the next station. Get law enforcement, backup, SWAT, someone on this train."

"We can only do so much. The train is due to stop in a few minutes. I'll see what I can do, but you might be on your own."

"Then I have to find them." He ended the call.

Oh God, if anything happens to them, I'll never forgive myself.

Where are you, Danielle?

NINETEEN

Danielle maneuvered through to the dining car and took a seat with Lucy, who was crying. Danielle comforted her the best she could, but all she wanted to do was get off this train. She asked the waiter for water but hoped the train would soon stop and then she and Lucy could flee for their lives.

She'd found a security guard dead. A train agency policeman lying in his own blood. Her blood had curdled. She'd thought to hide in an empty room, the door partially open, and that's when she spotted him. She didn't think the man who'd abducted them had done this.

That meant someone else was on this train.

Bottom line, she couldn't trust anyone she met on the train. She just had to keep her head down until the train stopped, and then she would race to the police at the train station. With everything in her, she wanted to go back and check on Reece. What had happened to him?

Had their abductor gotten the advantage and taken him out? Her body shook.

"Mommy?" Lucy lifted her head, her eyes and nose red.

Danielle's heart had shattered into a thousand pieces.

All she'd ever wanted was to take care of Lucy and give her a happy and healthy life. She'd failed miserably. She looked at Lucy.

Pull yourself together. You're going to make it through. Reece is going to live.

And then...you're going to tell him what you should have told him already.

"Yes, baby."

"You're shaking, so I know you're scared. I don't like for you to be scared. Please be happy. Like you always tell me, 'Calm down, Lucy. God is with you.' God is with us, Mommy. He sent Reece again." Then Lucy's eyes welled with tears. "Let's pray that Reece is okay."

Danielle laughed through tears—not tears of fear this time, but tears of joy. Her little girl was truly special.

"Okay, sweetheart. Let's pray." Danielle and Lucy prayed and kept on praying as the waiter set two glasses of water on their table.

"Drink up," Danielle said. She drank the water as well, noting the train was coming to a stop.

She was about to walk off this train without Reece.

I hope you're okay... But if he was okay, then where was he?

Oh, Reece. And she didn't know if Reece was alive or dead. She wanted to go back and look for him, but if he was injured or, worse, dead, then going back would put them back in the wrong man's grip. For Lucy's sake, she had to keep them safe.

Danielle rose from the table and took Lucy's hand. "It's time to go."

She moved forward, but Lucy resisted. "Are we going to wait for Reece to find us?"

God, please let it be so. Danielle nodded. "Yes.

That's the plan. But we have to get off the train. He can find us then."

And she would find the police. Use someone's cell and call them. Something.

Danielle lifted Lucy and exited with other passengers. Enough of this. She tugged her wig and Lucy's off and stuffed them in the trash.

Danielle turned and almost stepped right into a beautiful woman with short, stylish brown hair. Danielle recognized her, but from where?

The woman extended her hand. "Jamie Blackwell. Are you okay? I was so worried about the two of you." She smiled at Lucy and moved a blond curl behind Lucy's ear.

"How did you—"

"There's no time. John has woken up. He told me everything, and now he's asking for you. I came as soon as I was informed you would be arriving here."

"But who told you?" Danielle hadn't even known she was getting off this train here.

"Special Agent Bradley's superior, of course. I had to go through a lot to find you, but I'm here." She gestured for Danielle to join her and ushered her forward.

Danielle moved slowly, as if in a dream, with the strange woman. Now she remembered. Jamie's picture was on some of the corporate literature on John's laptop. She was the president of AlphaGentronics. Danielle's skin tingled as warning signals went off in her head.

Danielle suddenly stopped. "I can't go anywhere with you. We need a police escort. Someone is after us."

Jamie's smile froze in place, and her eyes turned dark. She revealed that she held a gun in her handbag aimed at Danielle. "Let's go."

"No, Mommy, don't go with her. She's a bad guy, too."

Danielle hated how much this would ruin Lucy's innocence. Her trust in people. "Sweetie, she has a gun. I have no choice." She still didn't move and directed her next words to Jamie. "Whatever you think I know, that I have, I don't have it. You're wasting your time."

"I don't want to hurt you. I never meant for this to happen, but I need that information."

"We don't have it."

"Yes, you do." She held the gun higher. "Don't make me kill you and take your daughter away. She's already lost so much, don't you think?"

Danielle nodded and walked next to Jamie, the handbag rubbing next to her to remind her of the gun. To her left she spotted the train station police office. An officer stood next to the door and watched them. Danielle noticed another man watching. Help was here. The police knew. All she had to do was get away.

She pretended to stumble forward and shoved Jamie away. "Run, Lucy!"

Danielle ran behind Lucy as a shield. She turned in time to see Jamie pointing her gun at Lucy.

"No!" Danielle screamed and surged forward to cover her daughter.

Gunfire cracked in the distance.

Jamie stumbled forward and fumbled the weapon. She dropped to her knees, then fell forward. Reece stood a few yards behind her, aiming his gun.

He'd been the one to shoot her?

Lucy screamed, and Danielle held her daughter. Screams erupted all around them, including from her.

People fled as law enforcement—a SWAT team

as well as the train police—rushed forward and surrounded Jamie. Reece closed the distance and pulled
Danielle into his arms. "I was so afraid. So, so afraid."

"You're bleeding. Are you shot?"

"I put on a rudimentary bandage, and I can get it
taken care of later. But I had to make sure you and Lucy
were safe." He walked them away from the scene where
medics were attending Jamie Blackwell.

"Bradley." A SWAT guy drew Reece's attention and
waved him over to where Jamie was being lifted onto
a gurney.

Reece never wanted to relinquish Danielle again. Or
Lucy, but he handed them off to a female law enforcement officer and hurried back to where Captain Reeves
walked next to the gurney. The team had taken the helicopter to the next station to see this through.

Jamie's eyes appeared glazed over, but she looked
right at Reece. "Another bigger pharmaceutical giant…"
Jamie closed her eyes.

And Reece backed away while they tried to save her
life. SWAT would have tried to negotiate with her for
Danielle and Lucy's lives, but when Jamie had pointed
the gun at them, at Lucy specifically, Reece hadn't hesitated.

"Reece…" Danielle called after him.

He turned and moved back to where Danielle and
Lucy waited. Lucy held her arms out. He took the little
girl and held her to him, his heart bouncing around inside and sensations, emotions he'd never felt before he'd
met Lucy, but that were now becoming familiar, ping-
ing around in his chest. Man, he loved Lucy.

Danielle studied him and Lucy in his arms. What

was she thinking? He feared to even consider what her thoughts might be.

"What did Jamie say?" she asked.

"'Another bigger pharmaceutical giant.' Those were her exact words." He shook his head. "We're only going to get answers when John wakes up." He didn't want to say it, but he couldn't be one hundred percent sure that Danielle and Lucy were safe. Not yet. Not until they knew the truth.

She nodded, then her eyes widened. "When Jamie greeted us, she told me that John was awake. Do you think she was telling the truth?"

"One way to find out." Reece handed his cell over to Danielle. "Give him a call."

"I need to put my necklace on," Lucy said, "if we're going to see him."

Danielle opened up her purse and pulled the necklace out. "It was on the side table last night… When I saw that you were gone, and the note that I had to come meet you, I grabbed it. I knew you would want it. I just forgot."

"It's okay." Lucy smiled. "It's been a long day."

Danielle and Reece shared a look and both laughed.

"If John is awake, I want to get on a plane back to California."

Reece looked at Lucy, then back to Danielle. "Are you sure?"

"Both of us will be much better if we put an end to this once and for all."

Danielle called the hospital and asked for information regarding John. She got his doctor. She held Reece's gaze, and it looked like she held her breath, too. By the look in her eyes, he knew she'd gotten an answer.

"Thank you. We'll be there as soon as we can. Please tell him for me." Danielle ended the call and then collapsed against him in tears. "He's awake."

Reece held her and ran his hand over the back of her head, through her soft hair. *Thank You, Lord.*

Holding Lucy, Reece found one of the train agency's law officers and asked for a ride to the airport. On the way, Lucy sat between Danielle and Reece. Fortunately Danielle had all her identification in her purse. The man hadn't stripped her of that, at least.

"I hope Uncle John is going to be okay," Lucy said.

"Me too, sweetie. Me too." He pushed her tangled blond curls out of her face. "How are you doing? You doing okay?"

She smiled and nodded. "I was scared, but I kept praying you would come for us, and you did. I wish… I wish you were my daddy."

Reece had no idea how to respond. He searched her gaze. He had so many unanswered questions. *I do, too, Lucy. I do, too.*

All he could offer at this moment was a smile, then he patted her hand. He wished he was her father, too, and that she and Danielle were in his life. He'd tried to keep his heart from falling again, because he didn't want to hurt Danielle like he'd done before. He didn't deserve her for what he'd done. But now… All he could think about was getting them back to safety and in his arms. In the recesses of his mind and heart, he'd longed for a second chance with Danielle, and this time he wouldn't walk away from her. This time he would want it to be forever.

At the hospital in California, Reece once again carried Lucy as they walked the hallways. At the door to John's room, he slowly opened it. Danielle rushed past. Reece set Lucy on the floor, and she dashed toward her uncle.

"Uncle John! Uncle John!" She almost crawled onto the bed with him, but Danielle held her back.

"Careful, Lucy. He's still recovering."

He smiled and held his hand out to Lucy.

She took it. "Look. I'm wearing the necklace, Uncle John."

His smile never faltered, but his gaze moved to Danielle. "I'm so sorry about everything."

"Do you remember what happened?" she asked.

"Not much after you arrived at the campsite. The police questioned me earlier, then explained that I'd been shot. I'm sorry to put you through being there."

Danielle glanced to Reece. "Um… Much more has happened since then."

Reece stepped forward, sensing that Danielle wanted him to broach the topic. No introduction was necessary, but John had to be curious about how Danielle had ended up with Reece again. He explained everything that happened from the moment he'd run into Danielle up to this moment at John's bedside. Maybe he should have held back and interrogated John. After all, he could play a criminal role in all of it. But they had waited so long for answers.

"So, we would appreciate if you would explain what's going on," Danielle said. She eyed Reece, almost a warning.

Both of them harbored anger toward John, but they had not heard his side of the story. Just how complicit was he, if at all?

John closed his eyes and remained that way so long,

Reece started to worry that he had fallen asleep. Or he was evading their questions.

When he opened them, they appeared more blood-shot. "Jamie is the president."

"We know her, Uncle John. She was a bad guy."

Danielle lifted Lucy in her arms. Maybe Lucy shouldn't be here for this, but then again, she'd suffered and should know the truth—even as a child. Plus, he was positive that Danielle wanted to be here for this, and neither of them was about to relinquish Lucy to someone else even for a moment.

John cleared his throat. "We were about to sell to Gannon Industries for billions. I had come across some damaging information. I collected data that shows that our new medical devices could be defective. Jamie didn't want that news to get out or the AlphaGentronics sale to Gannon would have fallen through. Jamie would have lost everything."

"And you, would you have lost?"

He nodded. "Yes. Everyone who stood to gain, of course, but only a few of us knew about the problem."

"Defective medical devices," Reece said. "What devices?" He remembered when he and Danielle had realized that John's company made Lucy's device. His heart raced while he waited for answers.

John frowned and closed his eyes, his features twisting in pain. "Pacemakers. I wanted you to come live with me so I could watch over Lucy personally. I… I didn't want to turn the information in about the defective devices—that would hurt us all. Bring down the company in the middle of the sale."

Danielle gasped.

Reece crossed his arms, though inside he wanted to wring this guy's neck.

"That's on me. I admit it sounds so awful as I say the words. But if you were living with me, and Lucy started to struggle, then I would put it out there for the world to know. I had a hard time convincing you to move out to live with me, so I worked with someone to develop a way to track Lucy and monitor her data. If you didn't live close to me, it was the next best thing. I would be more suspicious than Lucy's doctor, who might not immediately recognize a malfunctioning device, so I wanted this plan in place. I'm so sorry, Danielle. And I know I was breaking privacy laws, but I was worried about her. A few days ago, I demanded that changes be made to the devices or I would expose them."

"But they didn't agree to the changes," Danielle said. Her eyes had turned stone cold, all the warmth gone.

John held Reece's gaze—despair and regret filled his eyes. "That's when I ran into someone who attacked me. Wanted all the data, and then he tried to kill me. I fled to the campsite. Sent you that cryptic message to meet me. I thought we would be safe there."

"Those same people came after us. The man who shot you—Tim Blackwell—abducted us and wanted whatever he thought that you gave us." Danielle's voice cracked. "What did he think we had, John?"

"I'm sorry." He averted his gaze, tears forming in his eyes. "Tim wanted the information for himself to use against his wife. He couldn't divorce her because she held all the cards and all the money…unless he held something powerful over her. He wanted the information for his own gain. Jamie hired someone to retrieve it before Tim." John's eyes teared up. "I… I put you in the crosshairs. I couldn't have known."

"What were you going to show me that night before you were shot?" Danielle asked.

"I was going to show you some images of the pacemaker. I had them in my briefcase. And then tell you everything." He cleared his throat. "The guy I hired to set up Lucy's tracking, that's not all he did for me."

"You mean Greg Lewis?" Reece asked.

John nodded, a question in his eyes. "You know already?"

"He's dead," Reece said. "He was shot to death a few days before you were attacked at the campsite."

John's eyes widened, grief flooded them. "What have I done?"

"What did you hire the man to do?" Danielle huffed, growing impatient.

"I hired him to encrypt the data and put that in Lucy's medical record. Part of it is held in the memory of her pacemaker."

"What?" Danielle gasped. "John, how could you do this?" Lucy had crawled out of Danielle's arms and moved to a chair, where she curled in a ball. Danielle paced the room.

Reece ground his molars. "Why would you do that?"

"Mommy?" From the chair, Lucy looked at her mom for answers.

"It's okay, honey. I'm sorry for getting upset." Danielle frowned and stared at Reece. "I need to talk to John. Would you…would you take Lucy to get a snack?"

Reece needed to hear the information as well. "I think I need to be the one, Danielle. I'm the investigator on the case. And Lucy needs her mother right now."

Danielle stared at him, and he thought she might argue.

"Mommy, I'm hungry and thirsty. Can we go to the cafeteria and get those chicken fingers I like?"

"Okay, sweetie." She took Lucy's hand and started toward the door but turned to face John. "I'm glad you're awake, John, and that you're going to be okay. But we're going to have a long conversation about this when you're better."

"I know," he said.

Reece regretted letting Lucy be part of that conversation, but he couldn't have known just how bad it would get.

"How could you do this to your family?"

"I don't know. At the time, it seemed the safest place. Now I look back and hate myself, but I had no idea any of this would happen, or that Jamie would hire an assassin. How could I know that? If anything happened to Lucy, then someone would learn the truth when they looked into…"

"Lucy's death."

John groaned. "Oh, what have I done?"

Reece couldn't begin to answer the ramifications of John's decisions—he would turn this over to his superiors. He would have to recuse himself. He was too close to things now to make the right call. The lawyers would have to look at the timeline of events to learn if John's actions were part of duress and fear for his life.

And Reece had bigger concerns.

"So Lucy's pacemaker could be defective. We need to take care of her."

"The data is sent via the cloud to her doctor and he would notice if there were any anomalies, but as I mentioned earlier, her doctor might not recognize the malfunction until it was too late. I think it would be best if the device was replaced."

Fury boiled through Reece. John loved his niece and that was obvious, but in this decision, he had not put her first and had chosen to monitor her rather than risk losing money.

Reece would struggle to forgive him for hurting Danielle and Lucy in this way. "Let me be the one to share this news with Danielle. This is going to crush her, and…" He wasn't sure he could bear it.

"You love her, don't you?"

TWENTY

Danielle sat with Lucy at a table while she ate chicken strips. She had eaten worse the last few days than she had in her whole life. Danielle would have to remedy that and soon. But to be fair, they had been traumatized.

How could either of them move beyond what had happened—not just physically. The abductions. The near-death experiences. Houses blown up. Running from bullets. All of it. Danielle would have to move beyond it if she ever wanted Lucy to. And somehow she would have to forgive John. He had involved Danielle and Lucy in his company's bad business. So hard to believe.

She swiped the tears away. Her eyes would be puffy for a week after the last few hours of crying.

"Come on, sweetie. Finish up and we can head back up and see Uncle John."

"What about Reece?"

What about him? Now that this was over, Danielle didn't know about Reece. But she did know Lucy was going to be pining away for the man she'd already made her new father in her heart. Lucy loved Reece. Danielle stole one of Lucy's fries and chewed on it.

What about me? How do I feel about him? What if Danielle let herself count on him, love him again and he walked out on them for his job once more?

"We'll probably see him in John's room, and Lucy, baby, I want you to prepare yourself. You know we have to say goodbye to Reece. He's a police officer who was helping us to stay safe."

Lucy frowned, showing her displeasure with Danielle's response.

"I want him to be my daddy."

Yeah. Thought so. How did she handle this? A pang split Danielle's heart. She'd never told Reece. And if she did, then what? If he walked away—again, this time for different reasons—her heart would break. And so would Lucy's. And what if he wanted to be part of Lucy's life? How would that even work? Danielle and Lucy didn't live here. Lucy would be hurting for the father she couldn't see often. The questions without solutions overwhelmed her, and after everything that had happened, she had no idea what to think or what to say.

She only believed that she could not put them through the pain. Oh, why did the choices have to be so difficult and, in fact, no choices at all?

Tension from the days of living in fear, the emotional conflict she felt over Reece and how she felt about him, the fact that he was Lucy's father, built up until she could no longer hold it in.

Danielle couldn't help it. She pressed her face in her hands and let the tears flow. She held back the sobs. She'd prefer if she was at home and in the bathroom alone and she could just get it all out, but the floodgate had opened when she hadn't even thought she could cry anymore.

Oh, Lucy, I don't want to do this in front of you.

Lucy loved Reece, but there was the risk, too, that he might not want to step into the role of being her father—even if he learned he *was* her father.

"Mommy, I think you need to give Reece a chance."

The words of wisdom elicited a laugh in the midst of her sob. Danielle wiped away the tears and smiled. "How is it you're so smart for someone so young?"

Lucy smiled. "God made me that way. Besides, he's standing right behind you."

Danielle whipped around, and sure enough, Reece was a few feet away. She'd caught him in a half signal to Lucy. The two had been communicating while she was crying?

Reece held out his hand. "Let's take a walk."

She didn't feel like moving. Or facing John.

Lucy scrambled out of her chair and took Reece's hand. He thrust out the other one. "In the park. Let's go to the park. There's a nice one next to the hospital. We need to talk."

"Yeah, come on, Mommy."

Reece was going to make this harder for them. He was going to break their hearts.

Maybe Danielle could change that if…if she told him the truth about Lucy. If he knew, then maybe he could at least stay in his daughter's life, even if it was only now and then. Okay, Danielle would have to be more flexible about this. She had to prepare herself for what was to come. She put away Lucy's tray and then joined Lucy and Reece. They walked in silence down the hallway, out the doors and down a sidewalk on a beautiful sunshiny day. Birds chirped. Squirrels chattered.

Reece put Lucy on a swing and pushed.

Danielle stood next to him. Now was that moment of truth. Except… "What did you learn from John?"

"That he loves you and Lucy deeply. We have a lot to figure out and work out, and that's going to take time. Danielle…there's something you need to know."

"Reece, wait." Danielle stared at the ground. Then at the sky. How did she tell him?

He suddenly snatched her close and peered into her eyes. "I love you, Danielle. Don't…push me away. I know I hurt you back then. I broke both our hearts, but I was young and stupid. I love you, and I love Lucy. I want us to be a family. Please…" Desperation edged his voice.

She stared up at this man and saw the obvious love in his eyes. "I need to tell you something, and maybe once you hear it, you'll hate me and won't feel the same way."

"Nothing you could say would ever change how I feel."

She shrugged free. "Lucy is your daughter."

Lucy screamed and drew their attention. She flew out of the swing and landed on her feet. Then ran around and thrust her arms up to Reece. He picked her up.

"I knew it. I knew you were my daddy. I asked God to let you be my daddy. And this is the best birthday present of all!"

Reece kissed her on the forehead; he had such an endearing look on his face that Danielle had to admit what she'd known—she was in love with Reece all over again.

Then he stepped forward, placed his big hand at the back of her waist and tugged her close. He kissed her, long and thorough, as Lucy giggled.

"I have a mommy and a new daddy."

Reece ended the kiss, but stayed close, oh so close. "I've known for a while. Then everyone we ran into suspected it. I was just waiting for you to tell me, Danielle. I didn't want to push. But even if that wasn't the case, I love Lucy and I love you. I never would have wished the last few days on anyone, or the anguish you've gone through in losing a husband, but now our lives have intersected again. I know you're the woman for me. Lucy, too. If you'll have me. Will you marry me?"

"Yes!" Lucy pumped her fist.

"Now, hold on," Danielle said. "Not so fast."

She pressed her lips against his again, softly, but not so she couldn't speak. "I love you, Reece Bradley. So much I think my heart might burst. Yes, I'll marry you and we can be a family at last."

* * * * *

If you enjoyed this book,
pick up the previous books in Elizabeth Goddard's
Mount Shasta Secrets miniseries:

Deadly Evidence
Covert Cover-Up

Available now from Love Inspired Suspense!

Dear Reader,

I hope you enjoyed Danielle and Reece's story. I especially loved writing Lucy's character. She was such a special character for me, and I especially loved her faith in Jesus, her trust in Him and confidence that God was there for her. I hope and pray that you also have a childlike faith in God.

I love to connect with my readers. You can find out more about connecting and my books at my website, ElizabethGoddard.com.

Many blessings,
Elizabeth Goddard

**WE HOPE YOU ENJOYED
THIS BOOK FROM**

LOVE INSPIRED SUSPENSE
INSPIRATIONAL ROMANCE

Courage. Danger. Faith.

Find strength and determination in stories
of faith and love in the face of danger.

6 NEW BOOKS AVAILABLE EVERY MONTH!

Get 4 FREE REWARDS!

We'll send you 2 FREE Books plus <u>2 FREE Mystery Gifts</u>.

Love Inspired Suspense books showcase how courage and optimism unite in stories of faith and love in the face of danger.

FREE Value Over **$20**

YES! Please send me 2 FREE Love Inspired Suspense novels and my 2 FREE mystery gifts (gifts are worth about $10 retail). After receiving them, if I don't wish to receive any more books, I can return the shipping statement marked "cancel." If I don't cancel, I will receive 6 brand-new novels every month and be billed just $5.24 each for the regular-print edition or $5.99 each for the larger-print edition in the U.S., or $5.74 each for the regular-print edition or $6.24 each for the larger-print edition in Canada. That's a savings of at least 13% off the cover price. It's quite a bargain! Shipping and handling is just 50¢ per book in the U.S. and $1.25 per book in Canada.* I understand that accepting the 2 free books and gifts places me under no obligation to buy anything. I can always return a shipment and cancel at any time. The free books and gifts are mine to keep no matter what I decide.

Choose one: ☐ **Love Inspired Suspense Regular-Print** (153/353 IDN GNWN)

☐ **Love Inspired Suspense Larger-Print** (107/307 IDN GNWN)

Name (please print)

Address   Apt. #

City   State/Province   Zip/Postal Code

Email: Please check this box ☐ if you would like to receive newsletters and promotional emails from Harlequin Enterprises ULC and its affiliates. You can unsubscribe anytime.

Mail to the Harlequin Reader Service:
IN U.S.A.: P.O. Box 1341, Buffalo, NY 14240-8531
IN CANADA: P.O. Box 603, Fort Erie, Ontario L2A 5X3

Want to try 2 free books from another series? Call 1-800-873-8635 or visit www.ReaderService.com.

LIS21R